THE WHISPER MAN

By Stephen Leather

He's charming and good looking, he makes you laugh and he has a twinkle in his eyes. He's the sort of guy you'd be happy to spend time with. Until the moment when he asks you if you want to know a secret. You say yes, of course, and you lean towards him. That's when he whispers in your ear and everything changes. Within hours you are dead and your soul is gone forever. You've just met The Whisper Man.

When supernatural detective Jack Nightingale hears about a rash of suicides across London, he realises that it's more than a coincidence. Something has come from the bowels of Hell to wreak havoc in the world, and only he can stop it. But to do that he'll have to put his own soul on the line. And to make his life even more complicated, the police have found a book full of names of people who have been marked for death. And Nightingale's name is in it.

Jack Nightingale appears in the full-length novels Nightfall, Midnight, Nightmare, Nightshade, Lastnight, San Francisco Night, New York Night and Tennessee Night, and numerous short stories. The Nightingale timeline is complex; The Whisper Man is set between Nightshade and Lastnight, back when Jack Nightingale was in London working with his long-suffering assistant Jenny McLean and his nemesis Superintendent Chalmers was always on his case.

CHAPTER 1

Lucy Clarke looked at her watch. She was early and she hated sitting at a restaurant table on her own. There was a bar to her left so she walked over and slid onto a stool. A stick-thin barman with slicked-back hair flashed her a toothy smile and asked her what she wanted to drink. She ordered a glass of Pinot Grigio and looked at her watch again.

'Waiting for someone?'

Lucy turned to see a tall, dark-haired man sitting on the stool next to her. He was wearing a blue suit and a crisp white shirt with a blood red tie. She frowned. She was sure there had been no one on the stool when she had sat down. 'Two girlfriends,' she said.

He smiled, showing perfect, even white teeth. 'Ah, girls night out?'

'Once a month.'

His smile widened. 'Your husband lets you off the leash once a month? That's nice.'

'No husband,' she said. She held up her left hand and waggled her ring-free fingers at him. 'Not any more.'

'Footloose and fancy free? Excellent.'

He had eyes that were a blue so dark that they were almost black. She looked into them and her stomach lurched. She forced herself to look away and she fixed her eyes on her glass. 'Hardly footloose,' she said. 'I have a six-year-old daughter.'

'So you're a single mum? That must be challenging.'

'It has its moments,' she said. 'But I love Charlie more than anything in the world.'

'Charlie? So Charlotte? That's my mother's name.'

She looked back into his smiling eyes and felt herself falling into them. He reached out and took her right hand in his. 'Do you mind?' he asked, as he turned over her hand to reveal the palm. 'It's a hobby of mine.' His jet black hair fell like a curtain as he stared down at her hand. 'You're a happy person and you enjoy life, despite facing many challenges,' he said. 'You have been married and have one child.'

She laughed. 'I told you that,' she said.

'But your husband wasn't your first love. He was your second. No, third. But the two men you loved before him both hurt you and left you. You chose your husband because you knew he could never hurt you. You never really loved him.'

'Hey!' she said, and tried to pull her hand away but he held her tightly.

He looked up, smiling. 'I'm sorry, I didn't mean to offend. Sometimes I talk without thinking when I'm reading.'

'You read that in my hand?'

His smile widened. 'Of course.' He looked down at her hand again and she relaxed. He ran his finger across her palm and she shivered. 'You like dogs, but not cats. Your favourite colour is blue. You like to eat ice cream but you don't because you fear it will make you fat.' He looked up at her and grinned. 'It won't.'

'Can you tell my future?' she asked, her voice catching in her throat.

'Of course,' he said. 'Come closer. I have to whisper.'

'Whisper? Why?'

He winked. 'It's a secret.'

She leaned towards him and he put his mouth close to her ear. His voice was soft and comforting and she felt a warm feeling spread across her chest as he whispered to her. As he whispered, he put his hand behind her neck and drew her even closer.

Her eyes widened as she saw her two friends walk into the restaurant and go over to the greeter. Sally Willis and Laura McKay. Her two best friends. The greeter pointed at the bar and Laura waved over at Lucy.

'My friends,' she said, straightening up and pulling her hand away.

'No problem,' he said. 'Have fun.'

She slid off her stool and walked towards Sally and Laura. 'Sorry we're late,' said Laura.

Lucy looked at her watch. 'I was early.'

'And clearly making good use of your time,' laughed Sally, looking over her shoulder. 'So who was that?'

'Who was what?'

Sally grinned. 'You know who. The guy you were drinking with.'

Lucy turned to look at the bar. 'Which guy?' she asked.

'The tall good-looking guy who slipped out when you came over here,' laughed Laura. 'Come on, spill the beans.'

'I wasn't talking to anyone,' said Lucy. 'I was just waiting for you.'

Laura put a hand on her arm. 'If you want to keep him as your little secret, that's fine,' she said.

'Laura!'

The greeter came over. 'I'll show you to your table,' she said. Lucy looked over at the bar again, frowning. What on earth were her friends talking about? There hadn't been anyone there. Had there?

CHAPTER 2

Jack Nightingale sighed and looked up at the sign announcing the train times. The next one was due in two minutes but he was pretty sure it had been saying that for some time. It was just after ten so the morning rush hour was over and there were only a dozen or so people on the Tube platform. To his left was a workman in overalls holding a blue toolbox. Behind him was a middle-aged man in a suit who every few seconds looked at his watch and sighed through pursed lips as if the sound would somehow speed up the arrival of the train. A skinhead wearing a combat jacket and cherry red Doc Martin boots was leaning against the wall, glaring at anyone who looked in his direction.

Nightingale looked up at the sign again. Still two minutes. But as he stared at the screen, it changed to one minute. Maybe he wasn't trapped in time after all. A large Asian woman came down the platform in a brightly-coloured sari. She looked up at the sign, sighed and squeezed into a seat, putting her Marks and Spencer carrier bags on the seat next to her.

A group of young schoolchildren filed onto the platform, shepherded by two middle-aged teachers. The teachers had the pupils line up against the wall. Nightingale looked up at the sign. NEXT TRAIN APPROACHING. He looked at his watch; he had a meeting with his accountant at eleven and there was a client scheduled for one o'clock at his office. Business was slow and that was all he had lined up for the day.

He felt a breeze on his left cheek, signalling the train's imminent arrival. The blonde woman took a step towards the platform. Nightingale never understood why people didn't just wait for the train to come to a stop before crossing over the yellow line. She took another step. Nightingale was watching her openly now, wondering why she was in such a rush. Her third step was a little quicker. She had a Louis Vuitton hanging over her right shoulder and it was swinging freely as she walked. He could hear the roar of the train now, and the breeze was much stronger.

The woman took another step and she was almost running now. Now time really did seem to slow down for Nightingale. The woman was looking straight ahead, staring at the station wall on the far side of the tracks. Her face was a blank mask, her hands were lightly clenched. The wind was tugging at her blonde hair though she didn't appear to be aware of it. She took another step, her left foot crossing over the yellow line that ran the full length of the platform.

Nightingale opened his mouth to shout a warning, even though he knew he'd be wasting his breath. The sound of the train was almost deafening now. The woman planted her left foot and jumped, her face still blank. Nightingale grabbed for the scruff of her neck but she was already out of his reach. The brakes of the train screeched but Nightingale doubted it was because the driver had seen her. The train was still in the tunnel, but at the moment the woman left the platform it appeared and hit her. The sound was something Nightingale would never forget, a slapping sound like a wet towel being thrown against a wall and then she was gone and all Nightingale could see was the carriages whizzing by. The train slowed and came to a stop about halfway down the platform. The schoolchildren screamed and the teachers ushered them away. The train had stopped now but the door stayed shut.

'He pushed her!' shouted the Asian woman. 'I saw him! He pushed her!'

The Asian woman was standing up now. Nightingale shook his head. 'I tried to stop her.'

The woman pointed a blood-red nail at his face. 'He pushed her!' Her eyes were wide and bulging and her lips were curled back in a snarl. 'I saw him push her!'

'You didn't,' said Nightingale, backing away.

Hands grabbed his left arm and he turned to look at the teenage skinhead, a swastika tattooed on his neck. 'I've got him!' shouted the skinhead, his nails biting into Nightingale's arm.

'Get off me!' shouted Nightingale.

'He killed her!' shouted the skinhead.

Nightingale pushed him away with his free hand but then the businessman grabbed his other arm. 'Call the police!' shouted the businessman. 'Somebody call the police!'

'I was trying to help her!' shouted Nightingale, trying to get free. 'She jumped!'

'He pushed her!' shouted the Asian woman.

Half a dozen people were now crowding around Nightingale. Now matter how he struggled he couldn't get free. 'This is crazy,' shouted Nightingale.

The skinhead tried to head-butt Nightingale but the blow glanced off Nightingale's shoulder. Nightingale tried to move away but something tangled up his legs and he fell to the ground. Within seconds he was trapped under a pile of bodies, unable to breathe.

CHAPTER 3

They kept Nightingale in a windowless interview room with only a paper cup of water for company. There were two CCTV cameras up in the ceiling so he didn't light a cigarette, much as he wanted to. He had taken off his raincoat and put it on the back of the chair he was sitting on, and rested his feet on another chair. His chest and arms still hurt from the manhandling he had been subjected to on the Tube platform, and strictly speaking he was entitled to ask to be examined by a doctor but he was a big boy so he sipped his water and waited. The fact that he had once been a police officer cut him no slack, he knew that. Most serving officers hated their job and seemed to resent the fact that he had moved on to better things, though truth be told living hand to mouth as a private detective wasn't necessarily a step up, though at least he didn't have to worry that everything he said and did would fall foul of the Met's latest PC diktat.

He sat alone for three hours and had almost finished his bottle of water when the door opened and in walked Superintendent Ronald Chalmers, tall with greying hair and flakes of dandruff on the shoulders of his neatly pressed uniform. There was a younger man with him that Nightingale hadn't seen before, late twenties with thinning blond hair and wearing a grey suit that appeared to be a size too big for him. Probably a new detective, learning the ropes. Chalmers didn't introduce him. 'Get your feet off the chair, Nightingale, you're not at home now,' said the Superintendent.

Nightingale did as he was told. Chalmers used a handkerchief to wipe the chair clean and then sat down. 'So now you're pushing women in front of trains, are you?' said Chalmers. 'That's a new low for you.'

'I didn't push her, she jumped,' said Nightingale. 'I was trying to save her.'

Chalmers held up a hand to quieten him. 'Save your breath, Nightingale. We've reviewed the CCTV. You're in the clear.'

Nightingale sighed with relief. 'Why was that woman so convinced I'd pushed her?'

'You know how unreliable eyewitnesses are,' said Chalmers. 'Get five witnesses to a traffic accident and they won't even agree on the colour of the vehicles.'

'She'd have strung me up there and then,' said Nightingale. 'And those two guys who grabbed me were nasty pieces of work. I should sue them.' He stood up and took his coat off the back of his chair. 'So I'm free to go?'

Chalmers waved for him to sit down again. 'I've a few questions for you before you rush off.'

'I'm not under arrest?'

'Just sit down, Nightingale.'

Nightingale did as he was told. 'Can I smoke?' he asked.

'Of course you can't smoke,' he said. 'I'm sure you're aware of the Health Act of 2006, or are you developing early Alzheimer's?'

'If I'm doing you a favour by listening to you, I thought you'd cut me some slack and let me have a cigarette, that's all.'

'No slack is being cut, Nightingale. 'This lady who killed herself. Lucy Clarke. Do you know her?'

'Of course not.'

'Just ships that pass in the night?'

'It was morning, but yeah.'

'You didn't say anything to her? Or her to you?'

'You said you'd seen the CCTV.'

'The quality isn't great. And you did spend quite a bit of time staring at her.'

'Staring?'

'Staring. Looking. Whatever. So why were you so interested in her?'

Nightingale shrugged. 'She was pretty, I guess.'

'You make a habit of hitting on women on the Tube?'

'I didn't hit on her,' said Nightingale. 'I didn't even speak to her. I was bored, I was waiting for a train, she was easier on the eye than that horrible woman who started shrieking at me.'

'Did she look uncomfortable?'

Nightingale's eyes narrowed. 'What are you suggesting, Chalmers? That something I said made her jump in front of a train? You're clutching at straws, mate.'

'I'm not your mate, Nightingale,' said Chalmers. 'I'm a Metropolitan Police Superintendent investigating a suspicious death. So you need to keep a civil tongue in your head.'

'Suspicious? It's suicide, open and shut.'

'Lucy Clarke wasn't a typical suicide victim,' said Chalmers. 'She was stable, she was fit and healthy, no history of depression, and nothing had happened that would have caused her to kill herself.'

Nightingale shrugged. 'Maybe she just snapped.'

'There were no stressors, none that we could find.'

'Money problems?'

Chalmers shook his head. 'She was divorced three years ago and her ex-husband supports her and their six year old daughter. It was as amicable a divorce as you can get. He has been spoken to and has no idea why she would kill herself.' He wrinkled his nose. 'Did she look upset? Disturbed?'

Nightingale shook his head. 'She was your average Tube user, blank face and avoiding eye contact.'

'With hindsight, did she look like as if she had it planned in advance?'

'Do you mean, was she waiting to throw herself in front of a train?' Nightingale shrugged. 'I don't know. She was looking into the tunnel but everyone does that. Did she look tense? Not really, no more than anyone else.'

'So the train emerged from the tunnel and she just jumped forward?'

Nightingale nodded. 'It happened really quickly. By the time I realised what she was doing, it was too late.' He leaned forward across the table. 'Why are you so interested in a suicide?'

Chalmers looked pained. 'We've had a number of them over the past three weeks,' he said. 'Perfectly sane, perfectly happy people, just killing themselves with no warning, no notice, no reason.'

'No notes?'

Chalmers shook his head. 'No. And in all cases, they had something to do. They all had unfinished business. Lucy Clarke was on her way to get her nails done and was supposed to have collected

9

her daughter when school had finished. We had a guy two days ago who drank a bottle of drain cleaner and a bottle of bleach two hours before he was due to get a Waitrose delivery. Another woman made a FaceTime call to a friend to arrange to go for a drink, then went out onto her balcony and jumped to her death. Nine floors, so it definitely wasn't a cry for help.'

Nightingale sat back in his chair. 'People kill themselves,' he said. 'It's a fact of life.'

'Yes they do,' said Chalmers. 'But usually there's a history of depression or mental illness leading to it. Or there's a stressor involved. They lose their job or a relationship breaks down or they get diagnosed with an incurable illness. The suicides I'm talking about, there's no rhyme or reason. Perfectly well-adjusted, happy people are killing themselves.'

Nightingale frowned. 'And what do you expect me to do about it?'

'I was hoping that as you were on the spot, you might have seen something that would shed some light on it.'

'She seemed fine,' said Nightingale. 'She wasn't nervous, she didn't appear to be under any stress. Even as she ran towards the train she wasn't angry or sad, she was pretty emotionless.' His frown deepened. 'Come to think of it, her face was blank, pretty much.'

'Blank?'

'Expressionless,' said Nightingale. He leaned forward. 'Yeah, there was no expression at all. And considering she was about to throw herself under a moving train, that's not what you'd expect, is it?'

'I have zero expectations on this, Nightingale. I just want to know what's happening and if I can stop it happening again.'

'There are no connections between the victims?' asked Nightingale. He saw a look of contempt flash across the Superintendent's face and he held up his hands. 'I didn't mean to teach you how to suck eggs,' he said. 'I was just thinking out loud.'

'We checked, obviously. We even plotted their movements using their mobile phones and at no point were they ever less than half a mile apart. No family connections, no job connections, no connections, period.'

'So maybe it is just random? A statistical anomaly.'

'Yes, maybe.'

Nightingale could hear the lack of conviction in the man's voice. 'But if it's not, what are you thinking? That somehow one person is causing this to happen? A serial killer who makes his victims kill themselves?'

'I don't know what to think, Nightingale.' He looked at his watch. 'Okay, I've got things to do. You can push off.'

Nightingale stood up and put on his coat. 'Any chance of a lift back to my office?'

'About as much chance as hell freezing over,' said Chalmers.

CHAPTER 4

Jenny McLean looked up from her desk as Nightingale walked in. He was holding two Starbucks coffees but the peace offering didn't have any effect. 'Where have you been?' she hissed. 'I told you we had a client.'

'Helping the police with their enquiries.'

'You said you were going to see your accountant.'

'That was the plan.'

He put one of the coffees down in front of her, then pulled a Starbucks bag from his raincoat pocket and put it on her desk. 'Banana choc-chip muffin,' he said.

'You're still late,' she said. 'And Professor Dixon was on time. He's waiting in your office and he's not happy.'

'What's his problem?'

'Your tardiness, for one. But the reason he's here is his wife.'

'So a divorce job. Terrific.' He sipped his coffee.

Jenny got to her feet. 'You look like shit,' she said.

'I've had a rough day so far.' He sipped his coffee as Jenny flashed him a disgusted look before walking into his office. He followed her.

'I'm so sorry to have kept you waiting,' said Jenny to a middle-aged man with receding hair and wire-framed spectacles. 'Mr Nightingale was delayed.'

'Body under a train,' said Nightingale. 'Some people have no consideration.' He stuck out his hand. The man stood up and smiled showing uneven teeth. His skin was white and pasty as if he rarely saw the sun, and while Nightingale wasn't a man who cared over much about his own appearance, even he could tell that what was left of the man's hair seemed to have been cut by a man with vision problems and blunt scissors.

'Simon Dixon,' he said. 'Professor Simon Dixon.'

Nightingale smiled. 'Jack Nightingale,' he said. 'Private Detective Jack Nightingale.'

Dixon frowned at Nightingale's attempt at humour.

'Can I get you another cup of tea, Professor Dixon?' asked Jenny, flashing Nightingale a warning look.

'No, I'm fine,' he said, sitting down again. 'Three cups was more than sufficient.'

Nightingale put his coffee down on the desk, then took off his raincoat and handed it to Jenny. She looked at him disdainfully. 'Seriously?' she said.

'Please, would you mind hanging it up for me?'

She shook her head in annoyance and went back into the office while Nightingale sat behind his desk. 'So, my assistant tells me you are having marriage problems?' he said.

Dixon nodded. 'My wife is a witch,' he said.

'Yeah,' agreed Nightingale. 'It's a shame that more men don't find that out before the ceremony.'

Dixon frowned. He had a habit of constantly crossing one leg over the other, then reversing their position. Nightingale's finely honed detective skills deduced nervousness, and he was about to flash the man an encouraging smile when he spoke again.

'I think you misunderstand me, Mr Nightingale,' he said. 'I'm not complaining about Catherine's character. I mean exactly what I say. My wife is a practising witch.'

'A witch? As in flying around on a broomstick? Come on, Mr Dixon, wasn't that a film? Bewitched?'

'It's actually Professor Dixon. And I have heard of the film, and the TV series, but believe me, this is no comedy. I'm pretty much at my wits end and I need your help.'

Dixon seemed pretty young for a Professor, which might have accounted for his insistence on the title. Nightingale took a closer look at his face, perhaps he was a little older than his first guess, there were plenty of wrinkles round his eyes. Black bags under them too, as if he hadn't been sleeping well lately.

Dixon shifted in his chair, opened his mouth, closed it again and finally started to speak. 'It's going to sound ridiculous,' he said.

'I hear a lot of strange things,' said Nightingale. 'Just tell me. Start at the beginning.'

'Yes. Well, as I said, My name is Simon Dixon, I'm originally from Hastings, but I haven't been back there in years. It probably starts at University, which was where I met Catherine.'

'Which University?'

'Durham, we were both in the same college, but we never really met until our final year, and have been together ever since. She...we...she was the first woman I ever slept with. Still is. And I'm the only man she's...'

Even if it were true, Nightingale thought that was probably too much information. Though if it weren't true, it could be useful, depending on what it was Dixon actually wanted him to do. It seemed the man was getting to the point pretty slowly.

Jenny came back into the room and sat on a chair next to the door.

'We've been together ever since,' continued Dixon. 'All through University, then we both did Masters and PhDs, me in Anthropology and Catherine in European History. After that we managed to get lecturing jobs at the same University, Sussex. Quite a stroke of luck that two suitable vacancies turned up at once.'

Nightingale nodded, but said nothing. It was taking long enough as it was and he figured that asking questions would only slow things up.

'We did five years there, then had another stroke of luck. Two senior lectureships came up and we got them.'

'Same University again?'

'No, that really would have been a coincidence, but close enough. Mine was at Kingston, hers at Brunel. Close enough for us to buy a house in the middle.'

Nightingale was getting a little impatient now. 'Well, congratulations,' he said. 'But is all this relevant?'

'I had no idea at the time, but now I really think it is. On those days when I believe the whole thing.'

Nightingale had no idea what whole thing he might be talking about, but decided not to interrupt.

'We're both still there, but we've done very well. Catherine was made Professor of her department two years ago, the youngest ever, and I got my Professorship last year. Also the youngest ever at Kingston, as it happens.'

There was no mistaking the tone of pride in Dixon's voice, but Nightingale had congratulated him once and had reached his limit on ego-massaging. He nodded encouragingly, but Dixon had already begun speaking again.

'That's really when all this started,' he said. 'We went out and celebrated my promotion with some friends. Rather an expensive Chinese restaurant. We all had wine, then since we'd spent so much, the owner gave us a few rounds of Chinese liqueurs. I didn't fancy it much, but Catherine really liked it, she finished hers and mine too. On top of the wine, it was a little too much for her. She's never been that much of a drinker. Anyway, she was really quite squiffy, got rather affectionate in the taxi home. And then, when we actually got home, she wanted a nightcap. We have a cocktail cabinet, but it's usually only for guests. That night she had a brandy on top of all the rest. And that's when she told me.'

Most other men would have asked the obvious question when Dixon paused for effect, but Nightingale had done several interrogation courses when he was a cop and the rule was to always let the other person speak as much as possible so he just smiled and nodded.

'We were talking about how things had always seemed to work out so well for us, we'd always been so lucky. She laughed at that, and she said, 'Yes, it's like we have the luck of the Devil' or something like that.'

Nightingale leaned forward across the desk, looked straight into Dixon's eyes, and this time he did interrupt.

'Can you remember the exact words please, Professor?'

Dixon pursed his lips and nodded.

'I think those were the exact words, certainly about 'the luck of the Devil'. I said something about us having a very efficient Guardian Angel, and she shook her head. She said the Angels had nothing to do with it. I asked her what she meant, she was getting pretty far gone by then, but I remember her exact words this time.'

He paused again, but Nightingale wasn't biting. Dixon finally got to the point.

'That's when she told me that I had married a witch. 'You married a witch' were her exact words.'

'What did you say to that?'

'Nothing much. I'd had quite a few too, so I didn't take it seriously. I got her up to bed and we slept it off. I think it took me a couple of days to ask her about it.'

'And what did she say?'

'She laughed it off, or tried to. But there was a strangeness about her, the laughter wasn't genuine it seemed to me, and something about her didn't ring true. I know my wife very well, Mr Nightingale, or at least I thought I did.'

'So what did you do?'

'Put it out of my mind, it all seemed rather silly, and it wasn't as if either of us had achieved anything really out of the ordinary. Luck, certainly, but no lottery wins or anything like that. If she'd really been a witch, wouldn't she have gone for a film star or a footballer rather than a professor at a minor university? I'm a rational man, Mr Nightingale...or at least I was.'

There was obviously more to come, Nightingale needed a cigarette break, but didn't want to interrupt Dixon's story, so he forced the craving back down.

'But it made me more sensitive to good luck and happy coincidences. Happy for me anyway. Two months ago, the senior Professor in my department dropped dead of a heart attack in the middle of a lecture. Fifty-two years old, no history of heart problems. I got the job.'

Nightingale shrugged his shoulders. 'Happens all the time,' he said. 'People die. There was nothing suspicious about the death?'

'Nothing at all, as far as I know.'

'So what, then?'

'By itself nothing, though Dennis Jackson's death did create an opening for me. Not one I'd been looking for, or thinking about. I liked Dennis. And then...'

Another pause. Again Nightingale held his tongue. 'And then, four weeks ago, Catherine's head of department threw herself from the fourth floor of a multi-storey car-park.'

Nightingale's eyebrows headed upwards.

'Any reason?'

'None that anyone could come up with. She was happily married, with two grown-up children, no marital problems, no health or money worries.'

'And your wife is likely to get the position?'

'Confirmed last week.'

'But it's all just a string of coincidences. Have you mentioned it to your wife again?'

'Yes, several times in the last few months but she laughs it off. The same false laugh as before. Tells me not to be so silly.'

'So why are you being silly?'

'I've been doing some investigating of my own lately.'

'And? Broomsticks in the closet?' He smiled thinly when Dixon shifted uncomfortably in his seat. 'Joke.'

The Professor didn't show any sign of finding Nightingale amusing. 'No,' he said. 'We have a happy marriage in...er...every sense of the word, but Catherine is prone to insomnia, so she has her own bedroom for when she can't sleep and doesn't want to disturb me. She also uses it as overflow wardrobe space, she has a lot of clothes. I searched it when she was out. I really had no idea what I was looking for. I found it under the mattress.'

Again Nightingale didn't bite. Dixon was a master of the dramatic pause.

'It was a book, Mr Nightingale. A brown leather book, which seemed to have very old binding, but crisp new pages. Black pages. Each page had a name written on it in gold ink. And a date. The final name was Catherine's head of department, Sheila Fletcher. And the date was the sixth of last month. The date she died.'

'But that proves nothing, a list of names and dates.'

'Ordinarily I'd agree, except that I found that book four days before Sheila Fletcher killed herself.'

Nightingale frowned. 'Four days before? That does change things.'

'Yes. Though I didn't think of it at the time. It was only when I heard about her death that it became a connection.'

'Tell me about the other names and dates.'

'Well, there were a few I didn't recognise, with dates before I met Catherine. The first one that was familiar was my girlfriend from Hastings.'

'She died?'

'No, I still hear from her, she's married with two kids. But the date in the book was pretty much around the time she called me to say she'd met someone else.'

'Your wife knew her?'

'No, they never met, I've talked about her, but it was over before I met Catherine.'

Nightingale nodded. 'Go on,' he said.

'Some of the names after that I didn't know either. But there were people I'd worked with, some of whom took other jobs and left my way clear, I recognised the name of a woman who'd been on a short list for a lecturing job with me. The last name before Sheila Fletcher was Dennis Jackson, and it had the date of his death.'

'Your head of department?'

Dixon nodded.

'So, did you tell your wife you'd found the book?'

'Not at first. Once Sheila Fletcher died and I made the connection I took days thinking about it, trying to make a decision. It's not that easy to accuse the woman you love of being complicit in people's deaths. Finally I had it out with her two days ago. I told her I'd found the book, told her about the prediction of Sheila Fletcher's death, and I demanded to know what it was all about.'

'And what did she say?'

'She was furious and terrified at the same time, it seemed to me. She berated me for snooping, denied everything, but I just kept at her with it and finally she broke down.'

Nightingale waited again.

'She told me that it had been her great aunt who initiated her to the art, as a novice at just sixteen. Apparently the aunt had come over from Central Europe as a refugee at some time and had married an Englishman. She was initiated into a group near her home, though apparently she'd moved on and up in the system since then. Now she was with a much more powerful group and could use greater influence. To influence people in stronger ways.'

'To kill, is that what you mean?' said Nightingale. 'They were getting people to kill for them?'

'She swore that was none of her doing, the leader of the group just told her that things would arrange themselves, once they performed the ritual and the name was written in the book. She swore to me that after Sheila Fletcher's death she would never use it again. She was going to leave the group.'

'And you believed her?'

Dixon nodded.

'So what is this group?' asked Nightingale. 'Do they have a name?'

'That she wouldn't tell me for any amount of persuasion. Talking about it even obliquely seemed to drive her hysterical with fear. In the end I left it there, we both took a couple of sleeping pills and she went to sleep in the spare room.'

'And afterwards?'

'There was no afterwards. When I woke up she was gone. That was yesterday morning.'

'Had she taken luggage? Packed her bags?'

'Not that I could see. But the book was gone. At least, I haven't been able to find it.'

Nightingale frowned. He had about a dozen questions that were just itching to be asked. He settled on - 'Do you have any children?'

'No. We've been trying recently, but it hadn't happened. We've been thinking of making some appointments with fertility experts.'

Nightingale pressed on. 'Did you try her relatives?'

'She doesn't have any left, as far as I know. Her parents died in a car crash a year or so before I met her.'

'The aunt?'

'Long dead, apparently.'

'Have you called the police?'

'Yes, but they're not really interested. No sign of foul play, no history of abuse or irrational behaviour. Her car's gone too.'

Nightingale nodded. 'I'm guessing you spared them the bit about the book and the witchcraft?'

It was Dixon's turn to nod. 'Yes. They'd think I was insane. Can you help, Mr Nightingale?'

Nightingale was quiet for a few moments. 'I'll see what I can do,' he said. 'I can make a few enquiries about the book among some people I know, see if I can turn up anything, but there's no evidence of a crime, and I'm a one-man show, there's no way I can organise a nationwide search for one missing woman.'

Dixon lowered his head briefly, then looked up again. There were tears in his eyes. 'No, I suppose not. It was a forlorn hope, I'd seen your website a few weeks ago. She showed it to me actually, we had quite a laugh about it.'

'Laughed about what?'

'You know. The whole supernatural detective thing. Sorry, I didn't mean...I...I suppose I'd better go.'

He got up, and Nightingale stood up too. Nightingale handed him a business card. 'Look, Professor Dixon, if anything turns up you think I can help with or if your wife comes home and you'd like me to talk to her, give me a call. I'm sure it'll work out soon.'

'I hope so, Mr Nightingale,' said the Professor, heading for the door. 'I've just got an awful feeling that our luck is about to run out.'

Jenny let the Professor out and returned with her coffee and muffin. She sat down opposite him. 'You're not even going to try to help him? Couldn't you see how desperate he was, Jack?'

'Come on, love,' he said. 'What am I meant to do? I can't scour the whole of London for a missing wife with nothing to go on. The police will take it more seriously if she doesn't show up in a couple of days, and there are thirty-two thousand officers in the Met, last time I checked.'

If he'd expected that to placate her, he was due to be disappointed. Jenny flared her nostrils and widened her eyes. 'First of all, don't call me love, this is the twenty-first century. Second of all, how can you just walk away from this case? He's distraught, and we're talking about a woman who might be vulnerable.'

'She's a missing person, Jenny. And she has only been gone for one day. Okay, I can check with the police to see if she has been arrested, I can check the hospitals, and I can speak to friends and family. But that's all. If she was a suspected terrorist then we could get the police to check ports and airports and her phone and bank records, but she isn't.'

'You can get her phone checked. You've done it before.'

'That's getting harder than it used to be,' said Nightingale. 'The Data Protection Act means you can go to prison for sharing data, and the days of a mate in Vodafone helping me out in exchange for a drink are pretty much gone.'

'But what about the other business, the witchcraft thing?'

'Again, what can I do? All he's got to go on is a drunken conversation and a book with some names and dates in. Which only he has seen, and which has disappeared. Could mean anything, and it's no clue to finding her.'

'But if she really is a witch?'

Nightingale shrugged his shoulders. 'So what? The last hanging for witchcraft was over four hundred years ago, and it's not been illegal for sixty years in Britain. Plenty of people call themselves witches, Wiccans, pagans, whatever now. If you can think of anything constructive I could have done, tell me what.'

She sighed. 'Oh...I don't know. But you should be doing something.'

'I am,' he said. 'I'm going to drive down to the Travelodge in Hastings, to see if I can get some photos of the errant Mr Rigby with his secretary. That's the kind of case that pays the bills...and I take it we still have plenty of bills to pay.'

'You know we have,' said Jenny. 'That's why I think we should at least try to help Professor Dixon. He's not a pro bono case, he'll pay real money.'

Nightingale stood up and took out his cigarette and lighter. 'Okay, I'll see what I can do.'

'And why were you late? You said you were helping the police.'

'A woman threw herself under a train. I saw her do it. Chalmers thought I might have some insight into why she did it.'

'Oh that's awful.'

'It was a bit of a shock, but I'm okay now.'

'I meant for the woman,' said Jenny. 'Did she leave a note?'

'No note, no sign that she was unhappy. Chalmers says there's a rash of similar suicides.' He looked at his watch. 'I'd better be going. I'll probably go straight home after I've checked Mr Rigby out.' He opened a desk drawer and grabbed a small digital camera.

'Check the battery,' said Jenny. 'You know what happened last time.'

He checked and nodded. 'Good to go,' he said.

'And Jack, please don't forget about Mrs Dixon. I've got a bad feeling about her.'

'I'm on the case,' he said.

'Do you mean that?'

'Of course.'

'You're not just being glib?'

Stephen Leather

Nightingale sighed. 'Hand on heart, I'm not sure what I can do. But let me give it some thought. And that book Professor Dixon talked about is a bit of a mystery that I'd quite like to solve.'

CHAPTER 5

Nightingale was done with the Rigby case by nine o'clock. Mr Rigby was a romantic and so took his secretary to a local pizzeria for a pizza and a bottle of chianti before bedding her. Nightingale managed to get a table close by. He couldn't use his digital camera but managed to get several shots on his phone, including a beautiful one of Mr Rigby taking his date's hand in his and kissing it. He used the camera to get a shot of the two lovebirds entering the hotel and of the car in the car park. As Mr Rigby had assured his wife of eighteen years that he was attending a sales conference in Bristol, Nightingale figured she would have no problem in divorcing him, if that was what she wanted.

Nightingale had decided against driving to Hastings as there were several trains a day and his MGB had been playing up. The car had an intermittent electrical fault and some days just refused to start. As he walked back to the station he lit a Marlboro. He walked past a church where a priest was sitting on a bench at the entrance. 'Would you happen to have a spare cigarette?' asked the priest. He was in his sixties with curly grey hair and red cheeks that suggested a fondness for a good whiskey.

'Sure,' said Nightingale. He took out his pack and offered a cigarette to the man. The priest took it and Nightingale lit it for him. 'Busy day?' he asked.

'A wedding and three funerals,' said the priest. 'That's Hastings in a nutshell. You're not local, are you? I'm usually good with faces.'

'Down from London,' he said. 'Just heading back.'

'Business or pleasure?'

'The former.' Nightingale sat down and stretched out his legs. 'So where do you stand on suicide?' he asked.

'It's a bad thing, obviously,' said the Priest. He held out his hand. 'Ian,' he said.

Nightingale shook it. 'Jack. It's still a mortal sin, right?'

'I'm afraid so, yes.' The priest took a long pull on his cigarette and blew smoke up at the moon. 'Have you lost someone to suicide?'

'I was on a platform when someone threw themselves in front of a train,' said Nightingale.

'That's awful,' said the priest shaking his head. 'Truly awful.'

'Yeah, it pretty much ruined my day. And hers. So she goes straight to Hell, is that what the Church believes?'

The priest frowned. 'Are you a Catholic, Jack?'

'I'm not much of anything these days.'

'It shook you up, seeing her kill herself?'

Nightingale nodded. 'Very much so.' He drew smoke deep into his lungs and held it there.

'Did she have a family?'

'A young daughter.'

The priest tutted and shook his head.

'You didn't answer my question,' said Nightingale. 'She goes to Hell, right?'

'It's complicated.'

Nightingale chuckled. 'I hear that a lot.'

'The fifth commandment is clear, the taking of human life is a sin. And that includes taking your own life. All life belongs to God, no one has the right to end a life other than God himself. So yes, suicide is a sin. But is it a mortal sin?' He flashed a tight smile. 'That's where it becomes complicated. For a sin to be a mortal sin, three criteria have to be met. The sin must be gravely wrong, and yes, killing falls into that category. Then the person committing the sin must know that he or she is doing wrong. And thirdly, the sin has to be committed out of free will. Now, to go to Hell, a mortal sin must be unrepented. And the consequence of suicide is of course that there is no opportunity to ask for repentance. So on the surface, yes, suicides would go straight to Hell' He took another drag on his cigarette and this time blew smoke at the ground. 'But there are caveats. Most people who kill themselves do so in a moment of insanity. Not all, of course, but usually there is some element of mental imbalance and under those circumstances someone who kills themselves might not be aware of what they are doing.'

'Sort of an insanity defence, is that what you mean?'

'A soul should not be dammed to Hell for eternity because of a moment of madness,' said the priest. 'As I said, it's complicated. Suicide is the only sin for which someone can not repent, so it is a special case. But it isn't true that the Church turns its back on those who commit suicide. For a start, the Church does not have any power over who does or does not go to Hell. That decision is God's alone and the Church does not have the authority to question God's will. We are commanded by Christ not to judge others so we leave final judgment to God. He is the only one who can know what was going through the mind of the person who killed themself.'

'But I always thought that suicides couldn't have a Christian burial.'

'Then you thought wrong, Jack. The Code of Canon Law does not list suicide as a reason to deny a person a Catholic funeral or burial in a Catholic cemetery We can and we do pray for those who take their own lives. And we can have funerals for them, and they can be buried in our churchyards. I myself have buried two parishioners who took their own lives only last year.'

'What happened?'

The priest flicked ash onto the pavement. 'Sad story,' he said. 'They had been together for more than sixty years. Sixty-three, I think. Then they both got cancer. His was in the prostate, slow growing and the doctors said he wasn't to worry about it, he'd be dead of old age long before the cancer killed him.' He smiled apologetically. 'That's not how they worded it, but you get my drift?'

Nightingale nodded and took a drag on his cigarette.

'The wife got her diagnosis the same week, but hers was a more virulent form of cancer. She had a round of chemo but it hit her hard. The doctors wanted to try radiation but she said she'd had enough and wanted to die in peace. They sent her home and put the Macmillan people in touch with her. I went to see her many times. She suffered a lot, towards the end.' He shuddered. 'Then one evening I went around and no one answered the door. I had a bad feeling – a premonition maybe – and I called the police. They'd both taken sleeping pills.' He forced a smile. 'And champagne. I always thought that was such a nice touch. The husband had gone out and bought a bottle of Moet. They used it to wash down the tablets. They'd changed into their Sunday best.' He smiled again. 'I think they thought they'd just be buried as they were found, but of course life is never that simple.'

'The clothes were ruined?'

The priest nodded. 'Death is never pretty. Even if it's peaceful, everything is voided. But they were happy enough when they died. You could see it on their faces.'

'But they were Catholic so they knew that what they were doing was a sin?'

'They broke the Fifth Commandment, yes. But they died together and they died happily. As I said, it's up to God to judge them and I have faith that he'll judge them wisely.' He dropped the remains of his cigarette onto the ground and stubbed it out with his shoe, then got to his feet. 'I have to lock up,' he said.

'People steal from churches, even in Hastings?'

The priest chuckled. 'We've had to replace the roof lead three times in the last five years. It stopped when we alarmed the roof and put in CCTV, but I'm sure it'll happen again.'

'Nice talking to you anyway,' said Nightingale.

'Drop by anytime, Jack,' said the priest, then he turned and walked back into the church.

CHAPTER 6

Professor Dixon's head ached where he'd been hit, and his wrists burned where the ropes dug into them. He strained against the knots that held him, but it was useless. The figure in the grey, hooded cloak held the knife up once again, a mere six inches from his eyes.

The voice was soft, polite but insistent. An educated, well-spoken voice, patient, almost kind, though Dixon knew now that there was no real kindness in it. Not towards him anyway. 'Once more, Simon. I know what Catherine told you. That was a mistake and she'll be punished for it, but I cannot risk interference or my organisation being exposed. To whom else have you told your story?'

'The police. I told the police. They know all about you.'

'Hah. I hardly think so. I doubt you would have considered telling them anything beyond Catherine's...departure, it would have made you look a fool. Even if you had, they wouldn't have taken any notice. No, the danger to my plans may lie elsewhere, I shall ask again, but first perhaps a little...incentive.'

Dixon screamed, but there was no-one to hear it except his tormentor. He gasped in agony, and finally forced out the words. Nightingale. Jack Nightingale. He's a detective. His website says he specialised in unusual cases. I thought....I went, yesterday, I went there, but he wouldn't...he couldn't...'

'Hush now. Nightingale, yes, I have heard that name in another connection. He might certainly pose more problems than the police. If he were to be allowed to.'

Dixon groaned again, looked up at the figure in front of him and spoke again.

'Where is my wife? Please don't hurt her. I promise not to tell anyone, ever.'

This time the laughter was longer.

Stephen Leather

'Don't worry about your wife, she is in my care. And you are correct, you will not be telling anyone about us. Ever.'

'I promise, I promise. Please, let me go, I've told you everything I know, everything I did.'

'Of course you have. But this was never about information, Simon. You failed Catherine, and now is the time of reckoning.'

The knife was held up again.

The screaming was deafening, but there was nobody nearby to hear it.

CHAPTER 7

Jasmine frowned. Nice eyes and teeth but his jaw was just too wide. She swiped left. 'That's a no from me,' she muttered. She followed that rejection with another half dozen in quick succession. It wasn't that she was fussy, it was just most of the men on Tinder seemed to be dogs. Desperate dogs, at that. There were married men pretending to be single, poor men pretending to be wealthy, old men pretending to be young. Everyone lied. Though to be fair, Jasmine had spent ages choosing which pictures to put up and had stretched her profile description a bit. Telling prospective dates that her favourite thing to do was watching Netflix in her pyjamas with a pizza and a glass of wine was perhaps sending out the wrong message so she had gone with walking on the beach and horse riding.

'Ever found anything you like in there?' said a voice to her right. She jumped and almost dropped her phone. The stool next to her had been empty when she sat at the bar and ordered a glass of red wine. Now there was a tall, good-looking man in his early thirties sitting there. Definitely a swipe right, Jasmine thought. Dark blue eyes, neatly trimmed blond hair, unblemished skin and dazzling white teeth.

'Are you a model?' she heard herself ask, and her cheeks reddened.

He laughed. 'No, I'm real,' he said. He held out a hand. 'Simon.'

'Simon says,' she said, shaking his hand and wondering where her awful banter was coming from. What was she, twelve. 'Jasmine.'

'Nice to meet you, Jasmine,' he said, holding her gaze and her hand. His eyes were blue, but a blue so dark that they were almost black. She had never seen eyes that colour before. He was still holding her hand, she realised. His skin was soft but his grip was strong. His nails looked as if they had been manicured. He smelled good, but she couldn't identify the scent. There was a hint of orange there, and mint perhaps, and lavender, and something that reminded her of the way her father used to smell. 'You didn't answer my question?'

She took back her hand. 'Question?'

He nodded at her phone. 'Did you ever meet anyone worthwhile that way?'

She wrinkled her nose. 'Not really.'

'Anyone that you actually dated?'

She shrugged. 'I live in hope.'

'And the guy you're here to meet. You swiped him right, right?'

She tilted her head as she looked at him. 'How do you know that?'

'That you swiped right? If you swiped left, you wouldn't be meeting him.'

'How did you know I was here to meet a date?'

'Because if it was a boyfriend, you would probably have come with him. If you were here to see a girlfriend you would probably have got a bottle and a table.'

'Are you a detective?'

He flashed her his movie star smile. 'First I was a model, now I'm a detective? But I'm right, aren't I? You're here on a first date. With a man you met on the internet.'

She raised her glass in salute. 'You got me.'

'I hope it works out for you.' He waved at the barman. 'Whisky. A single malt. You choose. Two lumps of ice.'

The barman nodded and turned to look at a line of bottles.

'He'll choose Laphroaig,' said Simon quietly.

Jasmine looked over at the barman and sure enough he reached for the Laphroaig bottle and poured a measure into a glass. 'How did you know?' she asked.

'I'm good at reading people. It's my skill.'

'Your skill?'

'Or gift.' He smiled. 'Or curse.'

She laughed and sipped her wine, looking at him over the top of her glass. The barman dropped two cubes of ice in the glass and put it down in front of Simon. He nodded his thanks, picked it up, and sipped it. The smell of whisky reminded Jasmine of her father. In fact pretty much everything about Simon made her think of her father, dead now for more than ten years. 'Are you here to meet someone?' she asked.

'I'm always open to meeting new people,' he said. 'And I much prefer doing it in the real world.'

'So you hang out in bars, looking for women?'

He chuckled. 'I'm open to any opportunity,' he said.

'And you didn't tell me what you did. For a living?'

'Isn't that the strangest phrase?' he said. 'Asking people what they do for a living. As if their job defines their life. It always seems to me that if you're working, you're not living, right?'

'I suppose so.' He was very good at avoiding answering questions, she realised. Maybe that was another skill he had.

'And what do you do,' he asked. 'For a living?'

'I'm a student.'

'Nice.'

'And I work for Amnesty International,' she said. 'As a volunteer.'

'So you want to make the world a better place?'

'Of course. Doesn't everyone?'

He laughed and didn't answer the question. 'So you're good at reading people?' she asked.

'Oh yes, and not in a swipe right-swipe left kind of way. I usually have a good idea of what drives people, and of what holds them back.'

'Can you read me?'

He leaned closer to her. 'Of course,' he said. 'But do you really want me to?'

'I'd like to know what you think about me, yes.'

He smiled and held her look. 'I'll have to whisper,' he said.

'Whisper?'

'It's for your ears only.'

'Okay,' she said. She leaned closer and he put his arm around her shoulder. She could smell mint on his breath as he began to whisper in her ear.

CHAPTER 8

Nightingale smeared Colgate toothpaste on his toothbrush and bared his teeth at his reflection. He was quite proud of his teeth. No fillings, not too big, not too small, evenly spaced out. He gave his teeth a hard time what with his fondness for coffee and cigarettes, but other than a clean and polish every six months they needed very little work. He began to brush. His mind drifted back to what the priest had said about suicide. Nightingale had met dozens of potential suicides during his years as a police negotiator, and more than a few who had gone through with it. People in crisis, they were referred to in Met-speak. Nightingale doubted that he would ever consider ending it all but then he was reasonably young and in fairly good health. If one day he was old and facing a painful death, maybe he would take the easy way out. He finished cleaning his upper teeth and started on the lower ones. Young people killing themselves was something he could never come to terms with. When you were young, your whole life was ahead of you and death was final. It wasn't a video game where you started afresh. And what about the people who were left behind. How could parents possibly deal with the suicide of a child? And what about Lucy Clarke's six year-old daughter. How would she ever come to terms with her mother's suicide? Would a six-year-old even realise what had happened? Why would a mother kill herself knowing that she was leaving a young daughter behind?

Nightingale stiffened as he heard a sniff behind him. He whirled around but there was nobody there. He snorted softly. Of course there was nobody there. He was alone in the flat. He turned back to the mirror and began brushing again.

There was another sniff behind him. He moved his head slightly and in the mirror something moved. He stopped brushing and moved his head again. There was a blur over his left shoulder. He turned but there was no one there. 'Lucy?' he said. 'Is that you?' There was no response and he shook his head at his stupidity. He looked back at the mirror and this time he saw only his reflection. He smiled and his reflection smiled back. 'You're jumping at shadows,' he said to himself.

As he started brushing again he found himself thinking about Lucy Clarke on the train platform, the way her face had been a complete blank, devoid of all emotion, yet she had been determined to end her life. How could her life have gone so wrong that she wanted to end it all by throwing herself in front of a train? And why would a mother want to leave her daughter alone in the world? He heard another sniff behind him but he ignored it.

CHAPTER 9

Jasmine stared at the knife block. It was made of oak, with slots for nine knives. One of the knives was in the sink. She pulled out one from the back. It was a bread knife. She wrinkled her nose and put it back. The one next to it was a carving knife. It was rarely used. She and her two flatmates were more microwaved ready meals than Sunday roasts. The blade looked sharp, and it glinted under the overhead fluorescent lights.

She sat down at the kitchen table. She had a Cartier watch on her left wrist. The watch had belonged to her father and it was the only watch she ever wore. It was two o'clock in the morning. She didn't feel in the least bit sleepy. In fact, she didn't feel anything at all. Just numb. She put down the knife and undid the watch strap, then put it down on the table next to the knife. Why was the knife there? She frowned at it. She was supposed to be doing something. But what? She stroked the watch. She missed her father. She missed him each day from the moment she woke up and remembered that he wasn't there, until she closed her eyes to sleep and said a silent 'good night' to him. She looked at the knife and stared at her reflection in the cold steel. She looked pale. Like a ghost. She turned her right hand towards herself and looked at the thin blue veins running from her elbow into her hand. Veins or arteries? She could never remember. She placed the blade of her knife against the wrist. She missed her father so much. She closed her eyes and for a moment she thought she could smell him again. Orange and lavender and whisky. She opened her eyes and looked at the knife, frowning as if she was seeing it for the first time.

'Cut down, not across,' something whispered in her ear. She turned but there was nobody there. She looked back at the knife. 'And cut deep,' said the voice. 'Daddy's waiting.'

She twisted her wrist so that the point of the knife was pressing at the base of her left hand. She pushed and the blade went in. There was no pain, just the numbness. She drew the knife back, cutting deep, and blood oozed from the wound, then began to spurt as she severed the arteries. Or veins. She still wasn't sure which.

CHAPTER 10

On a list of people Jack Nightingale never wanted to see waiting in the street outside his office, the top three were the VAT Inspector, the Angel of Death and Superintendent Ronald Chalmers of the Metropolitan Police CID. The order of non-preference varied, but Chalmers certainly seemed to visit more often than the other two and had fewer redeeming qualities. Nightingale's heart sank as he saw the familiar figure of his least favourite policeman as he showed up bright and early, ready to start a day's work. Standing next to him was DS Dave Mason, whom Nightingale knew by sight, and had nothing against.

'What do you want, Chalmers?' he asked, with no trace of warmth.

Chalmers went for the same tone. 'It's Superintendent Chalmers to you, Nightingale. We need to talk.' He was in plainclothes with a dark overcoat that might have been cashmere over a dark blue suit. Mason had a cheaper coat and a grey suit.

'It's Mister Nightingale to you, Chalmers, and I've got nothing to say to you.'

'That's what you think. Anyway, it's up to you, we can talk here or I'll take you down the station.'

'On what charge?'

The Superintendent shrugged. 'I'll think of something. Outraging public decency with those shoes of yours?'

Despite himself, Nightingale glanced down at his latest Hush Puppies, which bore traces of several takeaways, regular Corona splashes and a fleck or two of ash. He sighed in resignation, and took the two visitors upstairs. For once he had beaten Jenny so he unlocked the office door and walked in, trying to give the impression he didn't care whether Chalmers followed him in or not. He hung his raincoat on the back of the door, then went through to his own office and sat down at his desk

Chalmers sat. Mason took a chair behind him and opened his notebook.

'Right then first things first,' he said. 'We had another suicide last night. A university student, good family, all set for a first at University College London, keen tennis player, worked for Amnesty International. She shared a flat with two other girls and according to them she was bright and cheerful and had everything to live for. Jasmine Macdonald. Do you know her?'

Nightingale shook his head.

'Do you need to check your files?'

'Jasmine is an unusual enough name. I'd have remembered. How did she kill herself?'

'She sat down at the kitchen table and used a carving knife to cut both wrists. Not little slashes either, deep cuts down the middle of the arm to the wrist. She bled out in seconds.'

Nightingale winced at the image.

'No note, no history of depression, just a girl who decided for no apparent reason to end her life.'

'And you think this is in some way connected to me?'

Chalmers sighed. 'No, I'm just clutching at straws but you were there at one of the suicides, I just hoped…' He shrugged.

'I was at the wrong place at the wrong time,' said Nightingale.

'What about Donna Moore? Is that name familiar?'

Nightingale frowned and shook his head. 'I don't think so.'

'She was sitting on her sofa watching Love Island and mid-way through walked over to the window and jumped out.'

'I'm guessing she didn't live on the ground floor,' said Nightingale.

The policeman's eyes hardened. 'Do you think this is funny?'

'I was trying to lighten the moment, that's all.'

'A woman died, Nightingale. She was on the ninth floor and we have half a dozen people who will be suffering nightmares for many years to come after they saw her hit the pavement. Miss Moore posted on Facebook a few hours before she killed herself. It was a bit strange. Something along the lines of "The Whisper Man tells it like it is, he knows how the world is, how it hates me and why I'd be better off elsewhere." About half a dozen of her friends replied, asking what had happened, but she didn't respond.'

'History of depression?'

Chalmers shook his head. 'The opposite. Life and soul of the party. So have you ever heard of this "Whisper Man"? You being involved in the spooky world.'

'Can't say I have, no,' said Nightingale. 'Two suicides isn't unusual, you know that.'

'We've had a lot more than two,' said Chalmers. 'Most are explainable. Depression. Family troubles. Illness. But including the two I've mentioned, we've had six recently. Two have jumped from tall buildings, one jumped in front of the Tube. Not yours, this was another.'

'Please don't call Lucy Clarke mine,' said Nightingale.

Chalmers held up an apologetic hand. 'One drank bleach. And drain cleaner. Jasmine is the latest.'

'And why do you think they're connected?'

Chalmers sighed. 'We've combed through the social media accounts of all the people who have died, and there's no mention of a "Whisper Man" anywhere else. But when the relatives were interviewed with a view to assessing the mental state of their victims, it became apparent that they had all met someone significant a day or two before they died.'

'Significant?'

'Three said they had met a good looking guy who had chatted them up. Another said she was in love. I can't help wondering if it's more than a coincidence.'

'Women meet good-looking men and kill themselves?' said Nightingale.

'I didn't say it made any sense, I just said it might be more than a coincidence,' said Chalmers.

'Coincidences happen,' said Nightingale.

'True. But people do have a habit of meeting unusual ends around you. I thought it was worth asking you about it.' He shuddered, then rolled his shoulders and steadied himself. 'Right, so tell me about Simon Dixon,' he said. 'And him I am sure you are aware of.'

'Who?' said Nightingale, feigning innocence.

Chalmers nodded and gave a long-suffering smile. 'Professor Simon Stanley Dixon of Larkrise, Beech Drive, Twickenham.'

Nightingale widened his eyes. 'He's dead?'

'Why would you say that?' asked Chalmers, tilting his head on one side.

'When a policeman gives you a middle name and address for somebody, it's rarely good news. I doubt the Met would send you round if he'd been done for littering.'

'You're not much of a comedian, Nightingale, never have been. Now once again, tell me what you know about him.'

'Why?'

'Because I'm a policeman, and I'm asking you. If you don't answer, I'm going to take you in for withholding information and ask you all over again in an interrogation room with a tape running.'

Nightingale sighed. 'What do you want to know?'

'You admit to knowing him?'

'It's not a crime to know someone. I met him once.'

'When?'

'Monday, here. Ten a.m. Until around eleven.'

'What did he want?'

'His wife had left him, he wanted me to find her.'

'So he was a client?' He pointed a warning finger at Nightingale. 'Do not fuck me around, Nightingale. Just answer my questions. Now, what services did you provide?'

'I said I'd be no use to him. Tracing a missing person is police work. He said he'd reported them missing, but the police weren't taking it all that seriously.'

Chalmers grunted. 'No evidence of a crime, not then,' he said. 'So, you turned him down?'

'Yeah. Not my kind of thing.'

Chalmers thought for a minute or so. Then he spotted the flaw in Nightingale's story. The man was an ass, but he was an experienced and competent detective.

'So, if he told you about his missing wife, and you said no, why did he stay an hour?'

Fair point, thought Nightingale. He hated lying, especially to the police, it always involved improvising, getting in too deep and trying to remember the stuff you'd fed them.

'Background, not that it was much help. He had no idea why she'd gone. Anyway, I don't swear to how long he stayed. I just schedule my appointments in hour blocks. Is the timing crucial?'

'Not on Monday,' admitted Chalmers. 'You never saw him again?'

'So, he's dead?'

'Why do you say that?'

'You said "never saw". If he was still alive it would be "haven't seen". Probably. I'm not really a grammar Nazi. Why don't you just get to the point?'

Chalmers sighed. 'Alright, he's dead. Found this morning when the cleaner let herself in. It wasn't pretty, apparently.'

'Murder?'

'Suspicious.'

'Cause of death?'

'I'm not here to discuss an open investigation with a civilian. I just wanted to know your connection with the man. Your name seems to come up in connection with a lot of dead people.'

'Allegedly,' said Nightingale. 'I don't remember ever being charged in connection with anything.'

'Not yet.'

'Anyway, what do you mean my name came up?'

'Two things. First of all your card was in his wallet, which was enough to set off alarm bells.'

'Well, now you know why.'

'The second thing was a little odder. Take a look, it's been dusted and analysed.' He took a book from his coat pocket and placed it onto the desk.

Nightingale frowned at it. It was a brown book, around the size of the average paperback, but bound in old, cracked brown leather. The front bore some characters he didn't recognise, and an embossed outline of a bird. He touched the cover briefly, and felt a tingling in his fingertips, as if an electric current had run through him. Was he becoming sensitive to the occult, or had he just imagined it?

He raised his eyebrows at Chalmers, who didn't appear to have noticed his reaction.

'I deduce it's a book,' said Nightingale. 'Does that help?' He was fairly sure that it was the book Professor Dixon had talked about, in which case he knew what he would see inside. Names and dates. Nightingale was getting a bad feeling about what was happening.

'Always the funnyman. Open it. Read it.'

'Is it okay to touch it?'

'It's not evidence,' said the superintendent. 'Not material evidence, anyway.'

Nightingale did as instructed. The pages were black, with a name and a date on each one, written in some kind of gold ink. He flicked through them all, not recognising any except the last two, but he kept his face expressionless when he read Dennis Jackson 24 October and Sheila Fletcher 6 February. Dennis Jackson had died leaving a job opening for Professor Dixon. And Sheila Fletcher was the woman whose job Mrs Dixon had taken. He looked up at Chalmers. 'A list of names and dates. Never heard of any of them. So what?'

'Keep reading.'

Nightingale turned the page. Simon Dixon, 7 March. 'That's yesterday,' he said.

'It is,' said Chalmers. 'His name and the date he was murdered.'

It was the first time Chalmers had admitted to it being a murder case. 'So what?' repeated Nightingale.

'Try the next page.'

Again Nightingale turned the page, and this time lost his poker face. The gold letters seemed to glow more brightly than all the others. Jack Nightingale 10 March.

'See what I mean, Nightingale?'

'I don't see anything, Chalmers. Except my name and a date. So what?'

'So we've done a little checking. Most of the people in that book we haven't traced yet, but the last three we have. Dixon, Fletcher and Jackson. Their names are in there against the dates they died.'

'So? Someone's morbid hobby. They're collecting dates of deaths. Like collecting car numbers, I suppose.'

'Maybe, but whoever wrote Dixon's date of death in there probably killed him. Nobody else could have known. As for you, maybe it's wishful thinking.'

'Well thanks for the sympathy, Chalmers. Anything else I can do for you?'

'Just turn the next page, Nightingale.'

Nightingale swallowed. He had a bad feeling about this. He turned the page.

Jennifer McLean 10 March. Nightingale said nothing, but looked up from the page and across at Chalmers, who had pressed his fingertips together and raised his eyebrows. Chalmers broke first. 'Well?'

'Well what?'

'Your name's in that book. So is your secretary's. Quite a few of the people in that book are dead, Nightingale. Maybe all of them. Looks to me like you're on somebody's "To-Do" list.'

'And that worries you?'

'Less than you'd think. I'd hate to see anything happen to Miss McLean though.'

'Ms,' corrected Nightingale automatically.

Chalmers ignored him. 'Suppose you tell me all about it, Nightingale. The whole Dixon business.'

Nightingale spread his hands, palms uppermost. It was meant to be a gesture of openness, but he doubted Chalmers would buy it. 'He came here yesterday to try to get me to find his wife. I said I couldn't help. He left. I've got nothing to add.'

Chalmers sighed deeply. 'Let's try it another way then, Nightingale. Where were you last night.? Let's say between ten pm and five am.'

'I was asleep.'

'From ten?'

'Okay, I was watching Sky Sports and then I slept. I was at home.'

'Can anyone confirm your alibi?'

'Oh come on, Chalmers. It's not an alibi. It's what I did. It's what most people do at night. They have a takeaway curry, they watch TV and they go to bed.'

'You had a takeaway curry?'

'Chicken chilli masala. And two poppadoms.'

'Rice?'

Nightingale shrugged. 'I'm trying to lose weight.'

'Delivery or did you collect it?'

'I picked it up myself.'

'Well for your sake let's hope they have CCTV. Give me the name of the restaurant.'

Nightingale gave the name and address of the curry house and Mason wrote it down.

'But even if you have an alibi, don't imagine we'll be leaving it there. This is a murder case.'

'Yes, and someone's trying to involve me in it. Now tell me Chalmers, how did he die?'

Chalmers pushed his lips in and out for a few seconds, then made his mind up. 'The post mortem's not been done yet. But the cause of death was a slit throat, there's no doubt about that. But somebody had given him a very thorough going over before that.'

'They wanted information?'

'Who knows, either that or pure sadism. But I'll tell you something, if they were after information, I'd bet my pension that they got it out of him.'

'That bad?'

Chalmers grimaced. 'Worst I've seen.'

Nightingale was about to reply when they all heard the sound of high-heeled shoes on the stairs, and Jenny opened the door. DS Mason stood up, but Chalmers stayed where he was, turned his head and grunted in her direction. Jenny's eyes opened a little wider as she saw the policemen, and she looked enquiringly at Nightingale. He said nothing, but waved her to a spare chair. She sat, straightened her skirt and gazed at Chalmers, who flushed a little. His tone was noticeably less hostile when he spoke. 'Morning, Ms McLean. A few questions, if you don't mind.'

The next hour saw Nightingale's blood pressure steadily rising. Chalmers took Jenny through the same questions he'd asked Nightingale, and Nightingale kept waiting for her to blow a hole in his story. Fortunately Chalmers missed a trick or two, by asking her if she could confirm Nightingale's account of Dixon's visit, rather than getting her to tell it in her own words. A few discreetly raised eyebrows from her employer, plus her own good sense, ensured there was no mention of the whole witch story. But there was nothing Jack could do to warn her about Chalmers's best trick. 'Would you take a look at this, Ms McLean,' handing her the book. 'Ever seen it before?'

She shook her head. 'No. What's it got to do with anything?'

'Open it please.'

'Chalmers,' said Nightingale, but the superintendent flashed him an angry look and wagged his finger.

Jenny turned the book over a few times, then opened the cover and started to go through the pages. She looked puzzled. 'Who are these people?'

'Some of them we haven't traced yet. The ones we have traced are dead.'

'My God, Professor Dixon is in here.'

'Yes.'

'And you, Jack...'

'I know.'

She stared at the page she'd just turned. 'Oh my God. Oh my God. It's me...'

Chalmers tried some more fruitless questions. Jenny had no idea how or why her name came to be in the book, no idea why anyone should want to kill Dixon, and had been nowhere near Twickenham the previous night. She'd been out to dinner in Central London, and the names of her dinner companions caused the policemen's eyebrows to shoot up in surprise. They hadn't expected her 'family friends' to come with titles, but it wasn't news to Nightingale. He'd often wondered why a woman who moved in the higher echelons of society chose to earn her living as assistant to a detective who was pretty much living from hand to mouth.

Eventually the superintendent ran out of questions. He jabbed a warning finger at Nightingale. 'This is typical of the weirdo nonsense you get mixed up in. None of it ever makes any sense, but there's always some poor sod ends up messily dead. I'm telling you now, you haven't heard the last of this by a long chalk. And if I find you getting in the way of my investigation, I'll have you locked up and the key thrown away.' He stood up and headed for the door, with Mason so close to his heels that when he stopped short Mason almost ran into him. 'If your unreliable memory manages to think of anything useful, or if you hear even a whisper, you'd better be on to me pretty damned quick,' said Chalmers, and he left with Mason following.

'Jack, he left the book behind,' said Jenny.

'Didn't he just.'

She frowned. 'It was deliberate?'

'Look, love, Chalmers is a complete disgrace as a human being, but he's a very experienced and successful policeman. There's no way he left that book behind by accident. He has no idea what it means, but he thinks I might be able to find out.'

'You don't think...'

'Yeah, in his rather clumsy, obnoxious, threatening way...he's asking for my help.' He picked up the book. 'And to be honest, I actually might be able to help him.'

CHAPTER 11

The battery on Nightingale's MGB had gone flat again so he caught a black cab to Camden and had it drop him close to Camden Lock market. The Wicca Woman shop was in a side street between a store selling bongs and t-shirts promoting cannabis use, and another that sold hand-knitted sweaters. The window display had changed since he had last visited and pride of place was now taken by a wooden chair on which were a dozen packs of Tarot cards. Nightingale pushed open the door and a tiny bell tinkled to announce his arrival. Alice Steadman was standing behind the counter, frowning at an ancient cash register. Nightingale had no idea how old she was, but if he had to guess he would have gone for late sixties. She had pointy bird-like features, wrinkled, almost translucent skin and grey hair tied back in a ponytail. Her green eyes sparked as she looked over at him. 'Why Mr Nightingale, what a pleasant surprise.' She was wearing a long black silk shirt and grey tights. She walked around the counter and silver bells on the toes of her slippers jiggled with every step.

She barely reached his shoulder as she smiled up at him. 'Is everything okay?' She touched him lightly on the arm.

'I'm fine.'

'Because usually you only visit when you have a problem.'

He grinned. 'You are my go-to person when I get out of my depth,' he said.

'Would you like a cup of tea?'

'I would love one, Mrs Steadman, thank you.'

She went over to the door and flipped a small sign from OPEN to CLOSED.

'You don't have to shut up shop for me,' he said.

'I don't have an assistant today and I need a rest,' she said. 'It's difficult to find good help these days.' She took him through a brightly-coloured beaded curtain into a small room where a gas fire was burning. She waved for Nightingale to sit on one of three wooden chairs around a circular table. She went over to a kettle on top of a pale green refrigerator and switched it on. She looked at him over her shoulder. 'Milk and no sugar,' she said.

'Thank you,' he said. Mrs Steadman had a razor-sharp mind and a memory that put his to shame.

She spooned PG Tips into a brown ceramic teapot. 'Your aura seems very disturbed, and I sense danger approaching you. Tell me about it.'

Nightingale explained about Professor Dixon and what had happened to him, and about the visit from Superintendent Chalmers and the book full of names.

When the kettle had boiled she poured water into the teapot and carried it over to the table on a tray with two blue and white striped mugs and a matching milk jug and sugar bowl. She sat down and poured tea for him, then added milk.

'Awful,' she said, when he had finished speaking. 'And you've brought the book, of course?'

Nightingale pulled it out of his raincoat pocket and handed it to her, but she flinched. 'No, no. Put it on the table, please.'

Nightingale set the book down on the table and Mrs Steadman picked a teaspoon and used it to move the book closer to her. She lifted the golden pince-nez on the chain round her neck and placed them on her nose, then peered nervously downward. She studied the engraving on the cover, then focused on the large bird. 'Oh my goodness. Oh dear, oh dear. How awful.'

'What's wrong?' asked Nightingale. 'I take it you know what it is?'

'Oh, yes. I can feel its vibrations from here. I really don't want to touch it at all; it would be most painful for me. It's a thing of pure evil. Don't you feel it?'

'Just a little tingle when I touch it.'

'Of course, you are not a sensitive. Not so much yet, anyway. Open the book for me, please.'

Nightingale opened the book, and turned the pages slowly, explaining the significance of the names he knew. Mrs Steadman drew in her breath sharply when he reached Professor Dixon's name, then shook her head vigorously when he opened the page with his own name. At Jenny's name, she gave a gasp of horror. 'Oh no, how awful. Close it please.'

Nightingale closed the book, and she put out one thin, claw-like hand and held it a foot above the book, shuddering all the while. After a minute, she pulled her hand back and slumped down back in her chair. 'Put it away again, please,' she said, waving at his coat.

Nightingale put the book back into his raincoat pocket.

'I am sorry, Mr Nightingale, you must think me such a silly old woman, but that really is very disturbing. You'll need to know about it, of course.'

'Please.'

'It's just that I've never seen such a thing before...never been in the presence of such evil...' She took a deep breath and sat bolt upright. 'Mr Nightingale, that is a Vlach Death Book.' She took another deep breath to steady herself. 'It's a very old tradition, which some say comes from Egypt, but which seems to have become most widespread in the Carpathian Mountains. The bird on the cover is the Carpathian Golden Eagle. In the folklore of the area, it is considered an Emissary of Death, which adepts can direct to destroy those who oppose them or stand in their way. Not literally of course, they don't use a corporeal bird. Rather they project a force. A killing force.'

'That can happen?'

'Oh yes, many traditions claim to be able to direct something similar. In the magic of voodoo for example, adepts use a doll to direct force against those they wish to harm.'

'And where are the Carpathian mountains?' Nightingale asked. 'I was never good at geography.'

'In central and eastern Europe, mostly in Romania from what I remember, and Poland and Serbia. Some other countries whose names have changed since I was at school.'

Nightingale wondered exactly where and when Mrs Steadman might have been at school, but stuck to the point. 'So what would the book be doing in Twickenham?'

'People don't always stay where they're born, particularly not these days, and when they move they can bring old customs and beliefs with them.'

'So how exactly would this book be used?'

'The name of the proposed victim would be written inside, with the date of...er...removal. On that date, the adept would hold a ceremony, make a sacrifice and unleash the force, the Eagle of Death.'

'You said sacrifice. What sort? Animal or human?'

Mrs Steadman shook her head. 'I don't know, I only have a vague knowledge of their traditions. They are rarely spoken about. The Vlach people were notoriously secretive, nomads with a strong belief in ancient traditions, especially in the afterlife, and claiming bonds with the dead as well as the living. '

'Is there anyone else I could talk to, maybe find out more?'

'Possibly, but I would need to speak to some of my contacts. I will call you as soon as I get any information that might help.'

'Thanks. But, our names are in there, does that mean we're brown bread on Friday?'

'Brown bread?'

'Dead.'

Mrs Steadman winced at the word. 'Not necessarily, but it does mean you're in terrible danger, both of you. And someone wants you to know it. I very much doubt the book was shown to you by accident. They wanted to send you a message.'

'Yeah, that occurred to me. So how do I stop it?'

'Well, the easiest way is to stop the ceremony from taking place at all. Even better would be to destroy the Master Book.'

'Master Book? This isn't the only one?'

'No, I think the adept, the sorcerer, would give one to each follower, with the names of their personal enemies in there. For the purpose of the rituals, a much larger book would be used, which would contain the names of all the enemies of the followers. And be used to direct harm at them.'

'Sounds nasty.'

'Yes, it certainly is. And you'll need to find them to stop it.'

'So, you're telling me I need to find some unknown Eastern Europeans and a big book, somewhere in Britain? That really is a needle in a haystack.'

She smiled. 'Well, it's not quite that bad, is it, Mr Nightingale? I think if you were to find Mrs Dixon that would be a good start.'

'Except I have no idea where she is.'

'Oh, I think I can help you there...'

She got up and walked across to an old, black wooded sideboard at the other side of the room. She opened a drawer and pulled out a large, square mahogany box, which she set on the table. It was covered in carved symbols, none of which Nightingale recognised, and the top had a large blue stone inlaid into the centre. She opened the lid, to reveal a tray, partitioned into twelve compartments. Each one held a large crystal, all of different colours and shapes, but all roughly the size of a pigeon's egg. Each one had a gold mount attached to the top, with a length of gold chain. Nightingale put out his hand to touch one, but Mrs Steadman tapped it away.

'No, no. They are all fully charged, and must only be touched by their partners.'

'Who are their partners?'

'That remains to be seen. Now, I want you to extend the index finger of your right hand and bring it as close to each one in turn as you can, but without touching any of them. As you do that, I want you to try to picture a blue aura round your hand, and try to imagine projecting it around the stone. Can you do that? '

Nightingale had long since ceased to be surprised at anything Mrs Steadman asked, and so he simply nodded. He concentrated hard on projecting his aura, and brought his finger as close as possible to the first crystal, a vivid blue stone. He held it there for a full minute.

'Try the next one,' instructed Mrs Steadman.

It was the fifth one he tried when it happened. A large pink crystal. As Nightingale's finger approached, it seemed to pulse with an inner light, and he felt as if an electric spark had jumped from the stone to his finger. He flinched.

'That's the one,' she said. 'It has chosen you.'

'Lucky me.'

She gave him a reproving glance, lifted the tray of stones out of the box, and took one of several small leather bags out of the compartment beneath. She held it out to Nightingale. It looked incredibly old, but felt as soft and pliable as tissue paper. 'Put your crystal into the bag.'

He did as he was told. 'Thanks. How much do I owe you?'

'Nothing, the crystals sense their partners, they cannot be bought or sold.'

'Well thank you. But what's it for?'

'To the skilled adept, the crystal has a whole host of uses. One of the least of them is locating people.'

'And how does that happen?'

'Listen very carefully, Mr Nightingale. I shall explain.'

She did, for almost half an hour during which time she made a second pot of tea and opened a packet of Digestive biscuits. When she had finished, he thanked her and was about to put his newly-acquired crystal into his pocket. 'No!' she said and put up her hand.

Nightingale froze. 'What?'

'On no account must you put the crystal anywhere near that book,' she said.

'Why?'

'The crystal is a force of goodness. From the right path. That book is the complete opposite. If they come together there is no telling what will happen.'

'Like matter and anti-matter?'

'Something like that,' she said.

'Can I carry them together?'

Mrs Steadman winced. 'You can, but the further apart they are, the better. Under no circumstances should they come into contact with each other.'

'So different pockets of my raincoat would be okay?'

'I would prefer that you didn't carry them at the same time, but if that is necessary then separate pockets would be satisfactory.'

The book was in his left pocket so he put the crystal into the right. 'Mrs Steadman, what are your thoughts on suicide?' he asked.

'It's a very bad thing, obviously,' she said as she gathered up the tea things.

'Do you know what happens to people, after they commit suicide?'

She tilted her head on one side and looked at him quizzically. 'They die. I would have thought that was self evident.'

'To their souls, I meant.'

'It's complicated.'

Nightingale smiled. 'I seem to be hearing that a lot these days. So the souls go to limbo or purgatory? Not to Heaven? Or Hell?'

'Suicides often have problems moving on,' said Mrs Steadman. 'Generally they don't cross over right away. And often because of the way they die, they make their presence known.'

'As a ghost, you mean?'

'As a spirit,' she said. 'Sometimes it's because they still have things to communicate to their loved ones. But more often it's because the sprit needs to clear itself of negative thoughts, and to deal with the guilt.'

'Because taking life, any life, is a sin?'

Mrs Steadman nodded. 'And because of what they have put their loved ones through.' Her eyes narrowed. 'Do you have a reason for asking?'

Nightingale shrugged. 'I saw a woman kill herself recently. I didn't have time to stop her.'

'And now you feel a connection with her?'

'I'm not sure. But maybe.'

'That's perfectly possible. Was it a violent death?'

'She threw herself under a train.'

Mrs Steadman shuddered. 'That's awful. And yes, under those circumstances it is quite possible that the lady's spirit feels that you and she are connected.'

'We'd never met before that day.'

'No, but you were there when she passed violently. Have you seen her?'

'I'm not sure,' said Nightingale.

'You're not sure?'

'Sometimes out of the corner of my eye, but it's more just a feeling.'

'Feelings is how the recently departed stay in touch,' said Mrs Steadman. 'I wouldn't worry about it, really. It's probably her way of apologising for what she put you through. The feelings will pass eventually.'

Nightingale stood up. 'I hope so,' he said. He patted the pocket where he had put the crystal. 'Thank you for this. I'll put it to good use.'

'I'm sure you will. Just remember to keep it away from that awful book.' Mrs Steadman stood up and Nightingale followed her back into the shop. She changed the sign to OPEN and then looked up at him. 'Be careful, Mr Nightingale.'

'I always am, Mrs Steadman.'

She smiled but he could see the concern in her eyes. 'I have a feeling that something bad is going to happen.'

'A premonition?'

'Just a bad feeling.' She opened the door for him. 'I'll call you if I get any more information on the Vlach.'

Nightingale thanked her. He lit a Marlboro as he walked along the pavement. He had made light of Mrs Steadman's warning, but he too had a feeling of dread hanging over his head, a fear that something bad was about to happen. Something very bad.

CHAPTER 12

Jenny was at her desk studying her computer screen when Nightingale walked in. Her face fell when she saw he hadn't brought coffees with him. 'Much happen while I was away?' he asked.

'A couple of phone calls from people wanting their spouses checked out, I explained the costs and they both said they'd get back to me. Other than that, it's as quiet as the grave. And isn't that a cheery thought?'

Nightingale took the book out of his raincoat pocket and put it down in front of her. 'Good news, bad news,' he said.

'Wonderful,' she said.

'The bad news is that it's a thing. A Vlach Death Book. Once your name is in it, an eagle of death comes to kill you.'

'Mrs Steadman told you that?'

'She's by no means an expert, but she knows the basics. She'll ask around for more information.'

'And what's the good news?'

Nightingale took out the leather bag and emptied the crystal into his hand. 'She gave me this.'

She peered at the pink crystal. 'And that will what, protect us?'

Nightingale frowned. 'No. What? No. She showed me how to use it to find people. I can use it to find out where Mrs Dixon is.'

Jenny held up a hand. 'Let me stop you right there. The bad news is that an Eagle of Death is coming to kill us. The good news is that you have a lump of quartz?'

'Crystal.'

'Tomato, potato. Jack, what's the good news about the death book?'

Nightingale grimaced. 'Well, there isn't any yet. Not really.' He flashed her what he hoped was a winning smile. 'Mrs Steadman is on the case.'

Jenny slumped back in the chair. 'Tell me what she said.'

'Not much really. Just that there's this eagle and somewhere there's a more important book, a master book, and ideally we should find that.'

'Ideally?'

'Jenny, love, it sounds like mumbo-jumbo to me.' He held up the crystal. 'And this can help us find Mrs Dixon. I just need something personal of hers.'

'How are you going to get that?'

'I have a plan,' he said.

'What sort of plan?'

'Best you don't know,' he said. 'In the meantime I could do with a lift.'

'In the building? Why? Are you having trouble with the stairs?'

'Ha ha,' said Nightingale. 'To Gosling Manor. There's someone I need to talk to.'

'Who?'

'Lucy. Lucy Clarke.'

'Lucy Clarke? The girl who jumped in front of the train?'

Nightingale nodded.

'Please tell me you're joking.'

He shrugged. 'You're not joking, are you?'

He forced a smile. 'No.'

CHAPTER 13

Jenny brought her Audi to a stop in front of the gates to Gosling Manor. 'You really should get electric gates fitted,' she said.

Nightingale grinned. 'It's second on my list of things to buy when I win the lottery,' he said. He climbed out of the Audi, unlocked the padlock that chained the gates shut and pushed them open, Jenny drove through and he pulled them closed again. He got back into the car.

'And you need to get a gardener in to do something about the grounds. They're really overgrown now.'

'Third on my list,' he said.

'And what's top of this list, may I ask?'

'To give you a much-deserved raise,' he said. He pointed down the driveway. 'Home, James.'

She drove to the house and parked next to a massive stone fountain where a tousle-haired stone mermaid was surrounded by leaping fish and dolphins. Nightingale got out of the car and looked up at the two-storey mansion, stone making up the lower story with an upper floor of weathered bricks, topped with a grey tiled roof and four massive chimney stacks. He waited for Jenny to join him and then they walked together towards the ivy-covered entrance. The oak door was huge but it moved easily on well-oiled hinges. They stepped into the wood-panelled hall. Jenny looked around and wrinkled her nose. 'And a cleaner will be number four on your list?'

'Jenny, it'd take a team of cleaners a week just to dust this place,' he said. 'It's huge.'

'Then sell it.'

'I'll get around to it. Once I've worked out what to do with all the stuff in the basement.' He walked across the hallway to the section of the wooden panelling that concealed the entrance to the basement library. He pushed it open. There was a light switch just inside the panel and he flicked it on. The fluorescent lights below flickered into life. Nightingale went down the stairs first. Jenny followed him, holding on to the brass banister.

The basement ran the full length of the house and was lined with laden bookshelves. Down the centre of the basement were two parallel lines of tall display cases. There were two overstuffed red leather Chesterfield sofas at the bottom of the stairs, either side of a claw-footed teak coffee table that was piled high with books. Nightingale took off his raincoat and tossed it onto one of the sofas, then went over to the bookshelves. He ran his fingertips along a row of leather-bound books until he found what he was looking for. 'Here it is,' he said, pulling out a green leather-bound book with the author's name in faded gilt on the spine. It was a slim well-thumbed volume and the cover was scuffed from use. He took it over to Jenny and gave it to her. 'Chapter twelve,' he said. 'Dark Mirrors: Their Use And The Dangers Thereof.'

She frowned at him. 'Say what now?'

Nightingale walked over to a display case filled with crystal balls. Next to it was something covered in a back velvet cloth. He pulled the cloth away to reveal a mirror framed with old wood that had gone black with age. The frame was made up of dozens of carved animals. Jenny went over to get a better look. She saw a snake, a lizard, and something with six legs and claws. The mirror was pitch black, as dark as a pool of oil and she frowned as she realised there was no reflection. 'What is it?' she asked.

'A dark mirror. Sometimes referred to as a black mirror.' He rapped the back with his knuckles. 'In a regular mirror, the back is silvered. But for a black mirror they use black paint, or black tape. But for a real Satanic black mirror they use paint containing blood. Human blood.'

Jenny took an involuntary step back. 'Are you serious?'

He nodded. 'In the old days they used the blood from corpses taken from the gallows, the fresher the better.'

Jenny wrinkled her nose in disgust. 'That's awful.'

'It gets worse,' said Nightingale. 'To work best it needs to be blood taken from a criminal who's been executed. And the worse the criminal, the better. Child-killers and serial rapists would be preferred.'

She frowned. 'What do you mean, to work? What does it do?'

'It's used for scrying. When you use your inner eye.' He nodded at the book. 'It's all in there,' he said.

'Why are we here, Jack?'

Nightingale patted the mirror. 'We can also use it to talk to the woman that killed herself,' he said.

Jenny shook her head. 'There is no 'we' in this, Jack,' she said.

'Okay, I'll do it,' he said. 'I just need your help to move things around.' He grinned. 'And a lift back.'

CHAPTER 14

Andrew Maxwell sighed and frowned down at the selection of fresh fish laid out on ice. 'Seriously, you don't have sea bream?'

'We've got sea bass,' said the fishmonger, a balding man in his fifties whose expanding girth suggested that seafood wasn't a major part of his diet. Steak and kidney pudding and chips, maybe, thought Maxwell with a smile. Washed down with gallons of beer. And sticky toffee pudding to finish off. Maxwell regarded his body as a temple – the fishmonger's choice of venue was more likely a fast food joint.

'Sea bass has a totally different taste and texture, and the recipe I'm using calls for sea bream.'

The fishmonger shrugged. 'We're out,' he said. 'Sorry.'

He didn't sound the least bit sorry and Maxwell felt like giving him a piece of his mind but instead he flashed him a cold smile and walked away. There were plenty of other fishmongers in town, it's just that the one in Waitrose was convenient.

He carried his basket over to the vegetable section and began going through the pak choi. He knew from experience that the freshest produce was on the bottom so he rooted through the packets, checking sell by dates.

An arm reached by him, brushing against his shirt, and a well manicured hand picked up a pack. 'Sorry,' said a voice, deep and gravelly, it made Maxwell think of a cowboy astride a white horse, a six gun strapped to his waist. He had always been a fan of Westerns. The old ones from the Fifties and Sixties, with heroes like Randolph Scott and Jimmy Stewart. Not the Spaghetti Westerns featuring Clint Eastwood. Maxwell had never been a fan of facial hair.

Maxwell turned to look at the man and his stomach turned over. He almost gasped. He had the look of a young Pierce Brosnan, back in the day when he was on Remington Steele, square jawed with jet black hair and blue eyes that were so dark they were almost black. 'I see we're both fans of pak choi,' the man said. His accent was difficult to place. The north of England, maybe, but softened from years in London. A bit like Maxwell. He had spent his childhood in Bolton and couldn't wait to get away, from the town and from his family.

'My favourite Chinese vegetable,' said Maxwell, immediately mentally kicking himself for such a weak come-back.

'I fry it with garlic and chilli,' said the man, dropping two packs into his basket.

'I prefer soy sauce,' said Maxwell.

'Each to his own,' said the man. He held out his hand. 'Paul,' he said.

His grip was firm and dry and he looked Maxwell in the eyes as they shook. 'Andrew,' said Maxwell.

Paul held the handshake for a second or two longer than was necessary. He had perfect teeth, Maxwell realised. White and even. 'So, you live around here?' asked Paul.

'Not far,' said Maxwell. 'You?'

'Just visiting,' said Paul. 'But I'll be around for a few days. Maybe we could have a drink sometime. I know a place.'

'A place?'

'A bar. One of those pop-up speakeasy places, all mysterious and you need a password to get in.'

'Sounds awesome,' said Maxwell. 'I'm cooking for friends tonight but I'm free tomorrow.'

'That's a date, then,' said Paul and Maxwell's stomach lurched again.

'So where do I go?'

Paul smiled and looked around as if he feared being overheard. 'I can tell you the address and password, but I'll have to whisper it,' he said.

Maxwell grinned. 'I love it,' he said. Paul smiled and leaned closer, putting his lips close to Maxwell's ear. Maxwell could smell oranges and lavender and then a hint of mint. He shuddered with pleasure as Paul began to whisper.

CHAPTER 15

'I still don't think this is a good idea, Jack,' said Jenny. She was sitting on one of the sofas, watching him as she hugged a red velvet cushion to her stomach.

He looked up from the five black candles that he was placing around the mirror. 'It's a portal for viewing, that's all,' he said. 'Nothing can come through.'

'The book said that demons can move from their plane into this world through the mirror.'

'But I'm not contacting a demon,' said Nightingale. 'That's a whole different ballgame. I'm just trying to talk to a lost soul. It's the occult version of FaceTime.'

'What if something goes wrong?'

'It won't. But if it did, in the very unlikely event that it did, I just have to break off contact.'

'We've had problems with Ouija boards before.'

'It'll be fine,' he said. 'I promise.'

She nodded at the stairs. 'First sign of anything untoward and I'm up those stairs and into the Audi and I'm off,' she said.

'Agreed,' he said. He went back to setting out the candles. They were as thick as his arm with foul-smelling wicks that he thought probably had blood in them. He lit them one by one and the air was soon filled with acrid smoke. He picked up a copper urn of herbs that he'd mixed together from a selection of jars and bottles at the far end of the basement, following the recipe given in the book. 'Do me a favour and kill the lights,' he said.

'I'm not sitting in the basement of a spooky house in the dark,' said Jenny. 'I've seen enough scary movies to know that never ends well.'

'We've got candles,' said Nightingale. 'The mirror only works in candlelight.'

Jenny sighed in annoyance, then stood up and went over to a row of light switches. She flicked them off one by one and the overhead fluorescent lights went out. Eventually most of the basement was in darkness. Jenny stayed where she was, her hand lingering close to the switches.

Nightingale sprinkled the contents of the urn in a circle around the mirror and candles, then he put it down and moved closer to the mirror. He shivered. It was as if the mirror was sucking the warmth out of the air around it. He had placed the book on the floor in front of the mirror and he bent down to pick it up. He had marked the page he needed and he took a deep breath and composed himself. The words he needed to say were in Latin and he wasn't sure of his pronunciation but he had used the spell before without any problems.

'Ego astrum in speculum,' he began, but the words caught in his throat and he coughed. He took another deep breath and began again. 'Ego astrum in speculum,' he said. 'Vos ero tutus. Nusquam hic vadum vulnero vos. Deus vadum servo vos. Ego astrum procul speculum quod volo video vidi visum vos.'

He paused. The burning wicks spluttered and crackled. The air was thick with cloying smoke that was irritating his throat and he coughed again. The mirror was still impenetrably black. He coughed again, then finished reading the rest of the words. When he was done he closed the book and clasped it to his chest. He stared at the mirror, blinking away tears. At first there was nothing, just blackness, but then something moved. 'Lucy?' said Nightingale. 'Lucy Clarke.'

A grey shadow was swirling in the mirror, gradually taking on human form.

'I am here to talk to Lucy Clarke.'

'Who are you?' It was a woman's voice, Trembling. Uncertain. Scared.

'Is that Lucy? Lucy Clarke?' The shadow continued to coalesce. 'This is a safe place, Lucy. The light of God surrounds us. The love of God enfolds us. The power of God protects us. The presence of God watches over us. Wherever we are, God is.'

'Who are you?' asked the voice, stronger this time.

'My name is Jack. Is that Lucy?'

'Where am I?'

Nightingale bit down on his lower lip, not sure how to answer that question. The mirror was in the basement of Gosling Manor, but he really had no idea where Lucy was.

'Lucy, I was on the platform where you died.'

'You tried to stop me.' It was a statement, not a question.

'Yes,' said Nightingale.

'Thank you.'

'I'm sorry I couldn't prevent you from jumping.'

'So am I.' The figure was clearer now. It was the woman he had seen throw herself under the train, but now she was wearing a simple white robe.

'Lucy, what happened? Why did you kill yourself?'

'I'm sorry,' she said, She lowered her head and her hair swung across her face.

'You don't have to apologise,' said Nightingale. 'But can you tell me why you did it?'

'I had to.'

'Why?'

She kept her head down. 'He told me to.'

'Who? Who told you?'

She mumbled and Nightingale couldn't make out what she'd said.

'I can't hear you, Lucy.'

She looked up and for the first time he saw her eyes. They were brimming with tears. 'The Whisper Man,' she said.

'Who? What did you say?'

'The Whisper Man,' she repeated. 'He said he had something to tell me and he whispered to me and then I wanted to....' She shuddered and lowered her head again.

'What's his name, this man?'

She sniffed. 'I don't know.'

'How did you meet him?'

Another sniff. 'He sat next to me at a bar. He started talking to me and then he whispered and then I wanted to kill myself.' She slowly raised her head and looked at him. 'Can you help me?'

'I don't know,' said Nightingale.

'You have to tell my daughter that I'm sorry. And my husband. My ex-husband. Tell them I'm sorry.'

'I can do that,' he said.

'Tell them I love them and tell them it was an accident.'

'They know what happened, Lucy. They know what you did. The police will have told your husband.'

She wiped her eyes with the back of her hands. 'He made me,' she sniffed. 'The Whisper Man made me.'

'What did he look like, this man?'

'I don't know. He was just a man.'

'Tall, short? Fat, thin? What sort of hair did he have?'

'I don't remember,' she said, and sniffed again. 'All I remember is him whispering to me.'

'And what did he say, Lucy?'

'I don't know. I'm sorry.'

'You mean you couldn't hear what he was saying?'

Lucy shook her head. 'No. I remember listening and agreeing with him and feeling the words fill me up, but now, no, I don't know what he said.'

'Do you know why you killed yourself?'

She shook her head again. 'I had to,' she said. 'I don't know why but I know I had to.'

She peered over Nightingale's shoulder. 'Who's that?' she asked. 'Is there someone with you?'

'My associate,' he said. 'Jenny. She's a friend.'

'I have to go,' said Lucy, her voice trembling.

'Where?'

'I don't know.' She started to back away from the mirror, disappearing into the shadows. 'I just know I have to go. Remember to talk to my husband. Tell him I'm sorry.'

'I will do,' said Nightingale.

'And my daughter. Charlie. Please tell Charlie that I love her. That I will always love her. And that I'm sorry I won't be there to take care of her but that her dad is a good man and she'll be okay with him.'

'I will,' said Nightingale.

'Promise me,' she said tearfully.

'I promise,' said Nightingale, but she had already gone.

CHAPTER 16

'What do you think's taking him so long?' asked Jeremy, gesturing at the door to the kitchen. 'I mean how long does a soufflé take?'

'You know Andrew, he loves to watch things rise,' said Simon, and he giggled.

Jeremy laughed and sipped his wine. 'And what do we all think of the sea bream?'

'Overcooked,' said the third man at the table. His name was Johnnie and he was the youngest of the group, barely out of his teens. 'One might even say flaccid.'

'He does his best,' said Jeremy. 'But he'll never be Cordon Bleu.'

'I did like his pak choi,' said Simon.

'I do love Chinese,' said Johnnie.

'Don't we all darling?' said Jeremy, and they all laughed.

Jeremy sipped his wine, then called over at the kitchen door. 'Andrew! Do you need help with the microwave?'

The other two men laughed. They waited but there was no reply. 'Andrew!' Jeremy called again. 'Is everything all right in there?'

There was no response and Jeremy put down his glass. He stood up and went over to the kitchen door. 'Andrew?' he said, and knocked. He reached for the door handle, turned it slowly, and eased the door open. The moment that he opened the door, the smoke alarm burst into life and Jeremy leapt back. Johnnie and Simon laughed and Jeremy flashed them a rueful smile. He opened the door wide. Smoke was pouring out of the oven and he could smell the soufflé burning. He took a step into the room, his eyes watering, and that was when he saw Andrew, sitting at the kitchen table. There was a carving knife sticking into his left eye and his face was covered in blood. He was still sitting, his hands hanging lifelessly either side of his chair. Blood had pooled on the table and was dripping onto the tiled floor. Jeremy took a step back, his stomach heaved and he vomited over the door.

CHAPTER 17

Jenny didn't say anything as she drove away from Gosling Manor. Nightingale sat with his arms folded and his head down, deep in thought. 'Thanks,' he said eventually.

'For what?'

'For everything, pretty much,' he said. 'For the lift, for working for me even though I know I can be a bit of an arsehole sometimes, for not asking me what the hell is going on.'

'I like to think I'm working with you, rather than for you,' she said.

He grinned. 'There I go, being an arsehole again.'

'It's part of your charm,' she said.

'Really?'

She shook her head. 'No.'

She overtook a petrol tanker, smoothly and efficiently, and as always he was impressed with her skill behind the wheel. 'So what the hell is going on, Jack?' she asked.

'I don't know,' he said. 'At the moment I'm winging it.'

'These suicides, do you think they're connected to the book?'

He looked at her. 'Do you?'

'Jack, I don't know what to think. But I am worried about Mrs Dixon's book. Your name is in it and so is mine, and as Chalmers said, people in that book tend to die.'

'It's just a book.'

She pulled a face as if she had a bad taste in her mouth. 'You more than anyone know that things aren't always what they seem. Professor Dixon had a bad feeling about that book and he's dead. And the date next to my name was tomorrow, Jack.'

'I don't for one minute think a giant eagle is going to come and get you.' He grinned. 'And if it does, just stay indoors.'

'You think this is a joke, do you?'

'I don't know what you want me to say, Jenny. Do you want me to stay with you tonight?' He held up his hand when he saw the look of disdain flash across her face. 'In a purely bodyguarding capacity,' he said.

'No, I've arranged to see an old friend at the Savoy, for drinks and dinner. Why don't you come?'

'I've actually got something to do. In Twickenham.'

'Twickenham?'

'Yeah. Do you mind dropping me there before you head off to the Savoy?'

'What are you up to, Jack?'

'I need to find Mrs Dixon. And to do that, I need something personal.'

'Why?'

'That's how the crystal works. The crystal that Mrs Steadman gave me. She taught me how to use it to find people.'

Jenny frowned. 'Why don't you use the book? That belonged to her.'

Nightingale shook his head. 'The book had bad vibrations, she said. They'll interfere. I need a photograph and ideally an item of clothing, something that she's worn, or a piece of jewellery.'

'So you're going to break into her house and steal something? Jack, are you crazy?'

Nightingale laughed. 'I think that ship has sailed,' he said. 'You yourself said the clock is ticking, we need to find the master book that Mrs Steadman talked about.'

'So you do think we're in danger? "It's just a book" you said. Now you've changed your tune.'

'Better safe than sorry,' he said. 'And if I do find her, maybe she'll tell me that book is a load of nonsense. Either way, I need to find her. So can you take me to Twickenham?'

'I'm not going to help you break into their house, Jack.'

'I'm not asking you to. Just drop me outside and I'll get an Uber when I'm finished.'

She sighed. 'If you get caught, you'll be in so much trouble.'

'I'm a professional. I'll be fine.'

'A professional what? Because the last time I looked at your CV it didn't have housebreaker on it.'

He laughed. 'Now I know you're not serious,' he said. 'I've never had a CV.' He patted his coat pocket. 'But I did bring my housebreaking tools with me, so I'm good to go.'

He settled back in his seat as Jenny drove to Twickenham in silence. Jenny was right. He had downplayed the book, because he didn't want her to worry. But according to Mrs Steadman the book was a very real threat and unless he did something there was every chance that they would end up the same way as Professor Dixon and the other unfortunates that had been listed.

They reached Twickenham and Jenny used her SatNav to find Larkrise in Beech Drive. She parked five houses away. 'You're sure about this?' she said, looking at the house. It was a small detached mock Tudor building with an empty driveway and the lights were off.

'I'll be fine,' he said. 'You go and enjoy your dinner.'

'Come and join us when you're done.'

'Okay, I will.'

'And if you do get caught, please don't tell the police I drove you here.'

'Mum's the word,' said Nightingale. He got out of the Audi, blew her a kiss, then walked to the house. He heard Jenny drive away as he walked around the side of the building. He stood against the back wall of the house, and considered his options. There were some large kitchen windows, a set of French windows, which presumably led to the sitting-room. Along the side of the house there was a frosted window, probably a downstairs toilet, and the back door, wood with some smaller frosted windows, and a Yale lock.

He chose the back door, and went to work with a glass-cutter on the pane nearest the lock. He made quick work of it, and made sure it fell into his gloved hands rather than onto the floor inside. He reached through the hole, turned the knob of the lock inside, and slowly pushed the door open. This was the time it could all go pear-shaped very quickly. If the Dixons had an alarm, and if the police had reset it after leaving, he'd need to be getting out before he got in. The last thing he needed was to give Chalmers the chance to pin a burglary charge on him.

His luck held.

There was enough light coming through the kitchen windows for him to find his way into the hallway and along to the sitting room. The thick blue curtains were drawn so he flicked the lights on. It looked as though the SOC officers had taken whatever they needed, and cleaned up after themselves. He moved towards the display units at the far side of the room, flanking the TV and home cinema unit. The books were mostly the coffee-table kind, so he assumed there'd be a study somewhere for the specialist stuff. He darted his eyes along the shelves until he found four volumes with no titles at all. He pulled one down and opened it. He smiled when he saw that it was a photo album. He selected what looked to be the most recent picture of Mrs Dixon, standing by a swimming pool under a cloudless blue sky. He slid the photograph into his pocket and headed upstairs. On the landing, six doors stood closed. The third door seemed to be the bedroom that Catherine Dixon had used during her sleepless nights, if the nightie on the carefully made bed was any indication. Nightingale looked around for something suitable, but saw no jewellery box. He thought about the wardrobes, but it would be just his luck to pick something she'd never worn. Then his glance fell on the laundry basket. It wasn't the most tasteful thing he'd ever done, but he found what he was looking for.

He left the house, lit a cigarette and walked for ten minutes before calling for an Uber to take him to the Savoy.

CHAPTER 18

The taxi dropped Nightingale on The Strand and as he walked to the entrance of the Savoy, he lit another cigarette. 'Got a spare smoke, mister?' said a voice to his left. He knew who it was before he had even turned to look at her. She was wearing a black leather motorcycle jacket over a black t-shirt with a white ankh symbol on it. She was sitting cross-legged on a piece of cardboard. He could see fishnet tights and ankle-length black boots. Her hair was short and spiky and her make up was black. Black eyeliner, eye-shadow, and lipstick and her nails were also a glossy black. There was another sheet of cardboard propped up against her knees on which was handwritten in capital letters the words HOMELESS – PLEASE GIVE WHAT YOU CAN.

'Proserpine,' he said. 'Long time no see.'

There was a black and white collie with a black studded collar lying next to her and it growled softly. She reached over and scratched the dog behind the ear. 'Easy boy,' she said. 'He won't be here long.'

'That sounds ominous,' said Nightingale. He took out his pack of Marlboro and offered her a cigarette.

'I'm just stating a fact.' She took the cigarette. 'Thank you.' He reached into his pocket for his lighter but the end burst into flames and then settled into an orange glow. She took a long drag on the cigarette and then blew smoke into the air. It formed a perfect pentangle, held steady for a few seconds, and then dispersed in the evening breeze.

'Do you want to come in for a drink?' he asked.

She chuckled. 'With the lovely Miss McLean? I don't think so. When are you going to jump her bones, Nightingale?'

'She's staff. You don't mess around with staff.'

She grinned mischievously. 'Don't tell me you haven't thought about it.'

Nightingale shrugged. 'Thinking and doing are two different things.'

'In your world, maybe.' she said. She took another pull on her cigarette and blew another smoke ring, this one in the shape of an upside down cross.

'Now you're just showing off,' he said. The dog pricked up its ears and growled menacingly. 'No offence,' he said. The wind dispersed the cross. 'I'm assuming this isn't a social call,' he said.

'You're heading into dangerous waters, Nightingale.'

'The Savoy? One of the best hotels in the world.'

'You're putting your soul at risk,' said Proserpine.

'Last time I checked, my soul is my own.'

She smiled. 'It's so cute that you think that way,' she said. 'But we both know that your soul is mine, one way or another. You are going up against an enemy that has the power to take your soul, and you don't seem to be aware of the danger you are in?'

'The Vlach book? Is that what you're talking about?'

'The Vlach book can destroy your body but it will have no effect on your soul.'

'That's good to know.' Nightingale tried to blow a smoke ring but failed miserably.

'You need to take this seriously, Nightingale.'

'Take what seriously?'

'You have attracted the attention of a particularly nasty entity.'

'Well that wouldn't be the first time, would it?' He flashed a smile but he was trying to hide how worried he was. If Proserpine had come up from the bowels of Hell to deliver a warning, he would be stupid to not listen to her.

'Tread very carefully, Nightingale,' she said. 'You really don't understand how much danger you're in.'

'I'm listening,' said Nightingale. 'So there's a demon on my case, is that it?'

She shook her head with a look of scorn. 'No, he's not one of us. He's a bottom feeder. He takes souls wherever he can, but he's not part of any plan.'

'But you are?'

71

She wagged a warning finger at him, the nail sharp and pointed and as black as coal. 'This isn't about me, Nightingale. I'm just here to offer you some advice, whether or not you take it is up to you.'

'So what is his name?'

'He doesn't have a name. Or a sigil. So he cannot be summoned. He's a one-off, a glitch, by rights he shouldn't exist.'

'That doesn't make sense,' said Nightingale.

'Not to you, no, of course it doesn't.'

'Please don't use the earthworm trying to understand nuclear physics analogy, it's insulting.'

She shook her head sadly. 'You're not taking this seriously.'

'Because I don't understand what it is you're telling me. You can't even say what it is that I should be afraid of.'

'Because it can take your soul, if you allow him to get close. You don't do a deal with him, you don't summon him and tell him what you want and sign a contract and reap the benefits. He just takes.' She took a pull on her cigarette and blew a plume of smoke up at the night sky. It swirled and then solidified and formed itself into a serpent that hissed at Nightingale before dissipating back into smoke that was whipped away by the breeze blowing down the street. 'Your soul is mine, Nightingale. It has been since the day you were born. I am not prepared to allow him to take it.'

'I'm not going to kill myself, Proserpine.'

She shook her head sadly. 'You really don't understand, do you? He doesn't give you a choice. He'll whisper to you and what he whispers will make you kill yourself. That's what he does. He whispers and people die.'

'And what does he say?'

She shrugged. 'No one knows because everyone he whispers to ends up dead.'

'So I won't listen.'

She smiled. 'Well good luck with that,' she said.

'So what are you saying? I'm investigating these suicides so the demon responsible is going to come after me?'

'I already said he's not a demon,' she said. 'You need to pay attention, Nightingale. But yes, he will come for you.'

'Why? What's he got against me?'

'He knows you know about him.'

'How?'

She looked at him scornfully. 'Because he knows you've been asking about him. You used to be a cop, right? Back in the days when you had a real job. What would happen if you accessed the police data base to look at the file of someone of interest? Someone who was being monitored by other agencies?'

'The file would be red-flagged and someone would be informed that the file had been accessed.' His eyes widened. 'That happens in your world?'

'You sound surprised. But yes, when you – a mere mortal – start messing around with crystals or Ouija boards or dark mirrors, word gets around. So The Whisper Man will know you spoke to the woman who died. And he will come for you, Nightingale, you can trust me on that. He lives in the shadows and the last thing he wants is for you to shine a light on him. And if you let him whisper to you, you will lose your soul.'

'You keep saying 'he'. So it's a man, is it?'

'It's a suicide spirit, it can take any form it wants, but this one is usually a man. But its gender is self-determined, and he could just as easily appear as a woman if he wanted to.'

'You said it was a one-off. Now you're saying there are more of them.'

'They are each one-offs. Sometimes there is a glitch in the universe and they appear. Without rhyme or reason. Do try to keep up with me, Nightingale.'

'So this thing, it's The Whisper Man, right?'

'That's as good a name as any. If I told you its real name, it wouldn't mean anything to you.'

'And how do I stop it?'

'Stop it?' she repeated, frowning.

'How do I kill it?' he asked. 'What is its weakness?'

'When it's in human form, you kill it the same way that you would kill any human,' she said. 'But if you are close enough to kill it, it's close enough to whisper to you.' She shrugged. 'You need to drop what you're doing, Nightingale. If you leave it alone, maybe it'll leave you alone.'

Nightingale blew smoke down at the pavement. 'Thanks for the advice,' he said. 'It's good to know you've got my back.'

'As I said, I'm not prepared for anyone – or anything – to steal your soul from me.' She finished her cigarette and flicked the butt away. It hit the pavement in a shower of sparks, then morphed into a spider that scuttled away and disappeared down a drain. When Nightingale turned back to look at Proserpine, she and the dog had gone. The piece of cardboard was still on the ground. The words had changed, though. Now it read BE LUCKY, NIGHTINGALE. As he stared at the sign the letters began to burn and within seconds the cardboard was alight, burning fiercely and producing a thick cloud of black smoke. The cardboard was quickly reduced to ashes which were blown away by the wind.

Nightingale turned up the collar of his raincoat, smoked the last of his cigarette, flicked it into the gutter, and walked into the Savoy. The American Bar was to the left and he headed up a short flight of stairs. He stopped at the entrance to the bar and looked around. Jenny was sitting at the bar next to a good-looking guy in a dark blue suit that looked as if it had been made to measure. The man was laughing, showing perfect teeth, and as he reached over to touch Jenny's shoulder Nightingale got a glimpse of an expensive watch.

Jenny was laughing, too, and she didn't seem to resent the fact that he was touching her.

'Can I help you, Sir?' asked a porcelain-skinned girl with waist-length black hair.

'I'm here to see my friend,' said Nightingale.

The man moved his head closer to Jenny. She was still laughing. The greeter turned away to talk to a middle-aged couple who had just walked into the bar.

The hand was patting Jenny on the back now, and seemed to be gently pulling her towards him. Jenny's eyes were sparkling and she used her left hand to brush a stray lock of hair over her ear.

The man moved even closer. Then the realisation that he was about to whisper to her hit him like a punch to the solar plexus. He sprinted forward, his raincoat flapping behind him. The hand was bringing her closer to his face. His mouth was opening. Her eyes were widening and her lips were parting. Nightingale smacked into a table as he ran and it overturned and the two ladies sitting there shrieked in surprise.

The man started to turn to look at the source of the noise, but his hand continued to push Jenny towards him.

'Jenny, no!' shouted Nightingale. He reached the bar and grabbed the man by the scruff of the neck and hauled him off the stool. The man's arms flailed for balance and one of his legs buckled. Nightingale swung him around, drew back his fist and aimed a punch at the man's head. The man managed to get a hand up, deflecting the blow, but he fell backwards and hit the floor hard.

Jenny was staring at Nightingale, open mouthed.

'It's okay, it's okay,' he said, gasping for breath. 'You're safe now.'

He tried to put his arms around her but she shrugged him off. 'What the hell are you playing at, Jack?'

Nightingale pointed at the man on the floor who was staring wide-eyed up at them, his chest heaving as he panted. 'He's The Whisper Man.'

'What?'

'He's The Whisper Man, He whispers to you and you lose your soul.'

Jenny shook her head contemptuously. 'Jack, that's Matt Roberts, I was at uni with him.'

Roberts sat up and rubbed his chin. He stared up at Nightingale, a look of confusion on his face. Jenny hurried over to him and helped him up. 'Matt does part time work with the Samaritans, I thought he might be able to help us with some background on suicide.'

The greeter came up behind Nightingale. 'I'm afraid I'm going to have to ask you to leave,' she said. 'Sir,' she added as an afterthought.

'It was a misunderstanding,' said Nightingale. He turned to look at her and saw two big men in black suits standing behind her, arms folded.

'Obviously,' she said, and motioned to the door.

'It's okay,' said Roberts, rubbing his chin. 'Just some horseplay that got out of hand.'

'Well if you would take your horseplay outside, it would be much appreciated.'

Jenny slid off her stool. 'Emma, I'm so sorry,' she said. 'Please, I can absolutely guarantee that it won't happen again and that the boys will be on their best behaviour. And if we've caused any of your lovely guests any inconvenience I'll happily buy them a glass or a bottle of whatever they're drinking.' Jenny flashed the greeter a sweet smile that would have charmed a serial killer, and the woman sighed.

'Best behaviour,' she said.

'Cross my heart,' said Jenny.

She smiled at Jenny and nodded, flashed Nightingale a warning look, then led her two heavies away.

'How old are you?' Jenny asked Nightingale.

'I'm sorry,' he said.

'It's not me you need to apologise to,' said Jenny, sliding back onto her stool.

Nightingale held out his hand to Roberts. 'I'm so sorry,' he said.

'It's all good,' said Roberts. The two men shook. 'I suppose you were defending her honour.'

'No, it wasn't that,' said Nightingale.

'Good to know,' said Jenny.

'I mean, if I thought her honour needed defending, then of course I'd defend it,' said Nightingale. 'I thought you…' He left the sentence hanging as he looked at Jenny, wondering just how much she had told him.

'I've explained your theory to Matt,' she said. 'The bits that don't make you sound like a blithering idiot, anyway.' She waved at the stool next to her and he climbed onto it. Roberts took the stool next to Nightingale.

'Jenny says that you think someone is grooming people to kill themselves,' said Roberts.

Someone. Not something. So Jenny had been careful how much she had said to him. 'It looks like several people have killed themselves after talking to this guy,' said Nightingale.

Jenny waved over a barman and ordered Nightingale a Corona. 'No glass, he likes it au naturale,' she said.

'I'd suggest that's probably a coincidence,' said Roberts. 'People have been talked into suicide, I'm not denying that, but it tends to be a long, drawn-out process. Say someone is in a cult and the cult leader wants them to kill themselves, for instance.'

'Like Jonestown?' said Nightingale.

'Exactly,' said Roberts. 'More than nine hundred men, women and children died after their leader Jim Jones told them to drink cyanide. Some had to be forced to do it, but most did it willingly. But those people had been under his influence for years. I don't see that establishing that sort of control could be done in a day.'

The barman put Nightingale's drink down in front of him.

'Jenny says you were a police negotiator?'

Nightingale nodded. 'Yeah, in another life.'

'So you must have dealt with a fair number of suicides.'

'People in crisis they call them. Yes.'

'So you know the things that can drive a person to take their own life?'

Nightingale nodded again. 'Depression, a break-down in a relationship, money troubles, drug use. They're the main causes.'

'Exactly,' said Roberts. 'And from my experience it's usually a mental health issue at the centre, compounded by drugs or a stressor like a break-up or losing a job. Or with kids it could be bullying. But usually at the heart of it, there's a clinical issue.'

'You're not saying that only mentally ill people kill themselves are you?' asked Jenny.

Robert grimaced. 'Studies have shown that ninety per cent of suicides were suffering from depression.'

'I didn't know that,' said Jenny.

'You have to remember that the vast majority of the people who call out helplines don't kill themselves,' he said. 'They want to talk. The fact that they call shows that they don't want to die.' He looked at Nightingale. 'I'm guessing it's the same with you. If they hang around waiting for the negotiator to arrive, they're probably not that serious about doing it.'

Nightingale grimaced. He knew what the man was saying, and in the main he was correct, but there had been several occasions when people he'd been talking to had killed themselves. They hadn't been cries for help in any way, shape or form. 'Usually, yes,' he said.

'You hear what I'm saying, right? If someone was serious about killing themselves, they'll just do it. They'll hang themselves in the hallway of their house or they'll jump in front of a train or they'll get into a hot bath and slit their wrists.'

'Nice images, Matt,' said Jenny.

'Something like six thousand people kill themselves in the UK every year,' said Roberts. 'Most of the ones that do, don't ask for help. We get five million calls a year. Five million. That's one every fifty seconds or so. So the vast majority of people who have suicidal thoughts don't act on them.'

'Which is what makes this case so strange,' said Jenny. 'A guy talks to them and within a day they kill themselves.'

'A guy? The same guy?'

'We're not sure. But all the victims mentioned meeting someone shortly before they killed themselves.'

'We meet new people all the time,' said Roberts.

'I know, I know,' said Jenny. 'But one of the women called him The Whisper Man and made it sound like he was talking her into killing herself.'

Roberts pursed his lips. 'I can accept that someone can groom another person into killing themselves. Al-Qaeda and ISIS are something of experts in that field. But it takes time and the victim usually has to be susceptible in the first instance.' He frowned and rubbed his chin. 'How do they do it?'

'Two have jumped from tall buildings,' said Nightingale. 'One jumped in front of the Tube. One swallowed a bottle of sleeping tablets. One drank bleach. The latest is a student who slashed her wrists with a kitchen knife.'

'So six?'

'Six that the police know about,' said Nightingale. 'There could well be others.'

'And the woman who mentioned this Whisper Man? What did she say exactly?'

'She wrote about him on social media. She talked about meeting The Whisper Man.' He looked over at Jenny. 'What was it she wrote?'

'The Whisper Man tells it like it is,' said Jenny. 'He knows how the world is, how it hates me and why I'd be better off elsewhere.'

'Elsewhere?' repeated Roberts. 'Was she religious?'

'I don't know,' said Jenny.

'Maybe she thought she was going to heaven,' said Roberts.

'Except that suicide is a mortal sin,' said Nightingale. 'A belief in religion, Catholicism anyway, would work against suicide. According to the cops, several of the women who killed themselves met a man in the days before they died. A handsome guy, an interesting guy, something that attracted their attention. It could just be a coincidence.'

'Were any of the other five religious?'

Nightingale shrugged. 'I don't know.'

'Maybe Heaven is the wrong word to use,' said Roberts. 'Suppose they did all meet the same man. Maybe he was able to convince them that the next life would be better. In the same way that Muslims can believe that if they blow themselves to kingdom come they'll get seventy two sloe-eyed virgins in the next life.'

'I've never found a lazy eye attractive, myself,' said Nightingale.

'That's S-L-O-E,' said Roberts. 'Sloe. It means dark.'

'You'll have to forgive Jack,' said Jenny. 'He thinks he's being funny.' She punched Nightingale on the shoulder.

Nightingale raised his eyebrows. 'What?'

'Don't "what" me, Jack. Matt's a very busy man, don't play silly buggers.'

Nightingale put a hand on his heart and bowed at Roberts. 'My apologies,' he said.

Roberts laughed. 'My problem for taking you literally,' he said. 'That comes with being a Samaritan. You have to assume that everything said is the truth, or at least that what is said comes from the heart. And the honesty has to be a two-way street.'

'I have a strange sense of humour,' said Nightingale.

'No,' said Jenny. 'You have what passes for a sense of humour. That's not the same thing.'

'We won't argue about semantics,' said Nightingale.

'We won't argue at all because I'm right and that's the end of it,' said Jenny. 'Go on, Matt. You were saying?'

'I'm really just thinking out loud,' said Roberts. 'It could well be a coincidence. Plus suicides do tend to occur in clusters. Partly because of the publicity and the copycat effect.'

'Sure, but the cops know that. If they suspect that there's a connection, that's probably because there is one.'

'And you think this Whisper Man is the connection?'

Nightingale shrugged. 'Maybe.' He didn't know the man well enough to tell him about the dark mirror in the basement of Gosling Manor, or that he'd spoken to the spirit of the woman who had thrown herself under the wheels of a Tube train. And the fact that Jenny hadn't mentioned it, suggested that perhaps she didn't know him well enough either.

'I'm sorry I haven't been much use,' said Roberts.

Stephen Leather

Nightingale shook his head. 'No, you're helping me to get my thoughts straight,' he said. 'I'm maybe too close to the wood to see the trees.' He looked over at Jenny. 'We should eat. I'm starving.'

CHAPTER 19

Nightingale got back to his flat in Bayswater just before eleven o'clock in the evening. Dinner had been excellent and afterwards Jenny and Roberts had wanted a nightcap back in the American Bar. Nightingale had left them to it. There was something he needed to do.

He showered, twice, and changed into a white robe that had been dry-cleaned. He had cleared the furniture to the edges of his sitting room, and lit half a dozen white church candles that had been blessed by a priest.

The small leather bag that Mrs Steadman had given him was on a chair, along with a recent photograph of Catherine Dixon and the item he had taken from her laundry bag. He removed his robe and carried everything to the middle of the room, where he knelt down. He untied the bag and took out the pink crystal, on its silver chain. The photo showed a tall smiling woman, who seemed about the same age as her late husband, leaning against a five bar gate somewhere in the country. He still wasn't proud of stealing her underwear. On the floor he'd placed a large road map of the southern third of England. From around Luton down to the South Coast, and from the Welsh border across to the North Sea. He placed Mrs Dixon's items in front of the map, closed his eyes, and said a short prayer, the crystal pressed between his palms. When he had finished he opened his eyes and let the crystal swing free on its chain. He pictured a pale blue aura around himself as he took slow, deep breaths. He began to repeat her name.

'Catherine Dixon, Catherine Dixon.'

Nightingale focused all his attention on the name and stared hard at the photo. He whispered a sentence in Latin, and imagined the blue aura entering the crystal, helping it to show the direction in which she might be found, opening his mind to an image of the woman and her whereabouts.

The crystal started to swing, slightly to the left, then heavily to the right. Nightingale moved his head in the same direction and kept repeating the name.

'Catherine Dixon, Catherine Dixon.'

The crystal kept guiding his hand to the right, then up a little, until it finally stopped and swung in a tiny circle over Norwich.

It was a start, but Nightingale would need to narrow it down a lot more than that.

But not tonight.

He went into the bedroom, flopped onto the bed and closed his eyes. There was a dull thumping sound coming from one of the flats upstairs. New tenants had moved in the previous week and they were obviously night owls, playing music and walking around and possibly assembling furniture until the sun came up. Three nights after they had moved in Nightingale had purchased a box of foam earplugs. He rolled over, fished the box out of his bedside table, and inserted a plug in each ear. He lay back on the bed and sleep came almost at once.

CHAPTER 20

Nightingale overslept and didn't wake up until ten. With the earplugs in he had slept right through his alarm. He phoned the office to tell Jenny that he was on his way in but it went straight through to voicemail. He showered, shaved, pulled on his suit and headed for the office. He stopped off for coffees and muffins because he knew she wouldn't be happy about his late arrival, but when he got there the office was locked. He opened up, sat down at her desk and phoned her mobile as he sipped his coffee.

'The mobile phone you have called is switched off, or not available.'

Could she be on the Tube? Seemed unlikely, but maybe her car was playing up. Nightingale glanced at the office clock. It was almost eleven o'clock. She was late. She was very late. And Jenny was never late, unless she'd told him she would be.

He tried the landline at her house, but gave up after ten rings.

He lit a cigarette and tried to think of what else he could do. He had her parents' number, but she'd said nothing about going up there, and he didn't want to worry them. After all she was only a couple of hours late. It seemed pointless to start looking up numbers and calling the few of her friends he remembered, if she was with them, she, or they would have phoned. He'd just got to the idea of calling local hospitals, when the phone on his desk rang, and he snatched it up.

'Jenny?'

'Jenny? No, Mr Nightingale, it's Alice Steadman. I promised to call.' She paused for a moment. 'What's happened to Miss McLean?'

'I don't know that anything has. But she hasn't come in this morning and I can't get hold of her. It's probably not important.'

There was another pause, and a long exhale. 'You don't believe that for a moment, do you?' said Mrs Steadman eventually. 'When a very reliable young woman suddenly becomes unreliable, it means something has happened. And her name was in the book.'

'You're right, of course,' said Nightingale. 'I need to find her, and quickly.'

'You do. Perhaps what I have to tell you can help.'

'I'm listening, and I've got a pen.'

'There really are very few people in England who might have any knowledge of the Vlach people and their occult traditions. They are notoriously secretive. The only one who would be likely to speak to you is a priest of the Eastern Orthodox Church called Father Mihail Tasić.'

She spelt it out and explained to Nightingale what an acute accent was.

'And where do I find him?' he asked.

'I'm afraid it'll be a bit of a journey if you want to speak to him in person. He runs the Church of Saint Sava, in Norwich.'

'Norwich? Now there's a thing.'

He told her about his session with the crystal and that Mrs Dixon might well also be in Norwich. He heard her suck in her breath.

'I don't like the sound of this, Mr Nightingale. You could be in a great deal of danger here. That book wasn't left by accident, they want you to know that you are in their sights. And I am very worried about Miss McLean.'

'Me too. Maybe I can do something about finding her first.'

'Oh do be very careful, won't you?'

'Aren't I always?'

Nightingale put the phone down without waiting for an answer, and looked up at the clock on the wall though the time had barely changed since he last looked at it. He tried her mobile and landline again, more out of hope than anything else, then fired up the office computer to check for any e-mails from her.

Nothing.

He went to her desk and opened the top drawer. There was a scrunchie there with some of Jenny's blonde hair and a gym card with a recent photograph on it. He took both and went home. Once again he'd performed the ritual with the crystal, but this time using Jenny's name, and the scrunchie and gym card. Once again the crystal stopped and circled near the East Coast.

Norwich.

He phoned Father Mihail Tasić who agreed to see him once he'd mentioned Mrs Steadman's name, then he threw some clothes into a bag, just enough for a day or so. Shortly afterwards his green MGB was heading down the A11 towards Norwich with all the speed Nightingale could get out of her. Normally he'd have been enjoying the drive, and the opportunity to get the car out of London, off the motorway and onto what he thought of as a 'proper' road. But today all he was conscious of was eating up the miles as quickly as possible.

One way or another, this would be over by tomorrow night.

CHAPTER 21

It was just after four when Nightingale arrived in Norwich. He headed for the city centre, parked the MG in the first multi-storey car-park he saw, and followed signs to the Tourist Information Centre in the Millennium library. Inside five minutes he was outside again, with a map of the city and its surroundings. He also had a list of guest-houses and hotels, not that it looked like he'd be getting much sleep. Finally, and most important at the moment, he had directions to the Orthodox Church of St Sava, about fifteen minutes walk away.

Nightingale's idea of an Eastern Orthodox Church involved domes, minarets and thin spires, so he was surprised to find himself in a quiet residential street, in front of a typical, small, English parish church. For a moment he thought he'd been given the wrong directions, but then he saw the board in the grounds giving the name of the church, a list of times of services in English and some other language he didn't recognise, and the name 'Father Mihail Tasić'.

The priest had said he'd be inside this church all afternoon, so Nightingale pulled open the main door and walked inside.

He stopped dead in surprise as he looked round. Every inch of the interior walls seemed to be covered in icons, hundreds and hundreds of paintings of what he assumed were saints, stretching up to the roof. There were the normal pews at the front of the church, but also, all round the walls, some unusual high armed affairs with backs and arm-rests, but no seats. Nightingale assumed that they were used by worshippers who stood during the services.

He walked down the nave of the church, towards a screen which ran the width of the church. The screen was also covered in icons, and had a small door on either side, with a much larger one, ornately carved and beautifully decorated, in the middle.

Even Nightingale's Hush Puppies must have made enough noise to be heard, and when he was within ten feet of the large door, it opened, and a man in black stepped out and raised a hand.

'Sorry, Mr Nightingale, no further, if you please.'

'No problem, I didn't mean to offend.'

'No offence given or taken. It's just that I am meant to bless you before you come through the door, and it's far easier if we talk out here.' He smiled and held out his hand. 'Mihail Tasić.'

'Jack Nightingale.' They shook hands and Nightingale sized him up. He looked to be around forty, an inch or two taller than Nightingale, dark haired with blue eyes ringed with laughter lines. He wore a long black robe, a stiff black hat and a large silver cross on his chest, hanging from a sturdy silver chain. Judging by his build and the strength of his handshake, the father kept himself in pretty good shape.

'You have a lovely church,' said Nightingale.

'Thank you. As you would probably guess from the outside, it used to belong to the Church of England, St Mark's, but they decided it was superfluous to requirements, so we were able to take it over. The interior, of course, is all ours.'

'I noticed. Very impressive. What are those strange chairs round the walls?'

'They are called "stacidia", mostly used by the older people now. The idea is that one should stand in the presence of God, but it's a tradition that not everyone clings to. It's quite normal to find pews as well in Western countries. '

'You have a decent sized congregation?'

'It keeps on growing, as more and more people come to Britain from Eastern Europe seeking work and a better life for their families.'

Nightingale nodded. 'Yes, my plumber's Polish.'

The priest gave a wry smile.

'Indeed, but Poland is not just a nation of plumbers. Nor are my worshippers all Polish, we have representatives from many countries. Doctors, teachers, professors, cleaners, engineers, nurses, and plumbers too.'

'Sorry. I didn't mean to be glib.'

'No offence taken. Now then, Mr Nightingale, Mrs Steadman said you had some questions for me, and an item to discuss. Do you have it with you?'

'Yes,'

Nightingale fumbled in his raincoat pocket, but the priest stopped him again with a raised hand. 'No, no. I should very much prefer that this thing not be brought out in my church. Give me a moment or two to take off my uniform, and we can go across the road for a drink.'

CHAPTER 22

The Angel pub was quiet at that time of the afternoon, and the two men took their drinks to an empty corner table. Nightingale would have loved a Corona, but decided to stick to coffee. The priest took a large whisky. Father Mihail had shed the robes, hat and large cross, and wore a dark suit with a clerical collar. He leaned towards Nightingale, and spoke softly.

'Tell me about it, Mr Nightingale.'

'Jack, please.'

'Sure, and call me Mike.'

Nightingale told him everything, from Dixon's appearance in his office to Jenny's disappearance from it. Father Mihail sat motionless and silent, the only sign that he was listening was the deepening frown on his brow. When Nightingale stopped speaking, he gave a heavy sigh. 'Show me the book,' he said.

Nightingale looked round, but nobody seemed to be paying them any attention. He took the book out of his raincoat pocket and slid it across the table. The priest looked at it carefully, but made no move to take it from the evidence bag. He felt the embossed designs on the cover through the plastic and grimaced.

'It looks like Vlach work to me,' he said quietly. 'I am not of the Vlach myself, at all. But I have made a study of their folklore. But this is not completely of their tradition.'

'Why not?'

'The ancient Vlach would have been illiterate, so the idea of the Death Book is a later addition, possibly from a different tradition. But it is hard to know.'

'Because?'

'Because the Vlach are obsessively secretive about their ways, particularly those very few of them who practise the dark arts. They would be prepared to kill to keep their secrets from outsiders.'

'Which is why my name and the name of my secretary – Jenny McLean - are in that book?'

Father Mihail shrugged 'That does seem odd. From what you say, you knew almost nothing, and certainly could have made no connection to the Vlach. Nor could Mr Dixon. It is hard to see how you could have presented a threat. It's only the fact that they left the book behind that has drawn you into this. It's almost as if they are giving you information, then planning to punish you for knowing it.'

Nightingale nodded. 'There's something in that,' he said. 'But why would they want to do it?'

'I would have no idea. But if they wanted you dead, and they have the power that legend suggests, it would be far simpler to strike you and Ms ...er...'

'McLean.'

'Strike you down without all the rigmarole, and certainly without the warnings.'

'Maybe there is more to it. Fath...Mike, you said you have no connection with the Vlach, except as an academic interest...'

'Pardon me, I didn't quite say that.'

'I thought...'

'I said I was not one of them, I'm of Serb descent, but my interest isn't purely academic. My wife comes of a Vlach family,'

'Your wife? But you're a priest.'

Father Mihail smiled. 'That I am, but not a Roman Catholic priest, Jack. There is no obligation on us to be celibate. But we only get one chance at it. I could not have married a divorcée, and if, God forbid, my Dana should die before me, I would not be permitted to remarry.'

'And she's a Vlach?'

'She comes from a Vlach family, though we met here in Norwich, three years ago. She's a nurse at the University Hospital. I'd broken my ankle in my last-ever rugby game. It made me see I was too old for it.'

'So she might know more about it?'

'No. She's made no study of traditional folklore, Jack. She's a twenty-first century girl. No more interested in spells and curses than the average British girl would be in four-hundred year old love-potions and milk-souring.'

'Might she know someone who did take an interest?'

'No, I wouldn't think so.. Her parents are dead, she's got a couple of cousins she never hears much from, but otherwise there's no great connection to her old home. Look.' Father Mihail took out his wallet and flipped it open to show Nightingale a photograph. The tall blonde in the photo was certainly not Nightingale's idea of a priest's wife. She was standing on a beach somewhere, wearing a skimpy red bikini and a beaming smile.

Nightingale wrinkled his brow a little, she seemed vaguely familiar. He couldn't place her though, probably looked like somebody he'd seen on TV. 'Not quite dressed for church,' he said.

Father Mihail nodded, but didn't smile at Nightingale's joke. 'No indeed. A fine woman, but she has no faith. Quite the opposite. Would you believe she has never even set foot in my church?'

'Is that common with the Vlach?'

'Not uncommon. They tend to pay lip-service to religion, though they are not always very welcome in church.'

'Why not?'

'They have a tendency to want to dance and sing during prayers. It upsets other worshippers.'

'It's happened here?'

The priest shook his head. 'I know of no other Vlach near here. They are not by nature gregarious. And do not often care to mix with outsiders'

'So do you hear any rumours about Vlach witchcraft round here?'

The direct question caused Father Mihail's frown to return, and he was silent for a moment. 'No, but I doubt that I would. If there are Vlach here, they would be unlikely to seek out a priest. As I said, they pay lip-service to the teachings of the Church, but their core beliefs are from a much older time. They have a deeply rooted belief in life after death. The dead are highly respected and they claim to have contact with them frequently to ensure the afterlife of their souls. And fortune telling, sorcery and witchcraft, whether for good or evil, are very strong traditions within them.'

Father Mihail was clearly warming to his subject, but Nightingale needed specifics. 'So what would be involved in the ceremony of killing me?'

'I did a little research after Mrs Steadman's call. The adept would need to perform a summoning ritual, to awaken the spirit of the

Carpathian Eagle. This would involve combining herbs and blood from a smaller bird, chants and summoning spells. Then the energy would be focused by rubbing a page of the book with something of yours, writing your name in blood and then a final invocation to unleash the killing spirit.'

'But not in this book?'

'No, that's by way of a talisman for the individual member of the group to keep. Names of people who stood in their way, but have been removed. The group would have a larger book, with many, many pages to contain all the names of those they had cursed, possibly over many decades. '

'How many enemies could one group have?'

'It's not just a question of personal enemies, there are tales of Vlach witches being paid by Nobles to kill their enemies, by businessmen to remove rivals.'

'So they could be working for someone else to kill me, and Jenny?'

'It's possible.'

'Dixon could have been killed by the Eagle spirit,' said Nightingale. 'But some of the others seem to have died natural deaths, even suicide.'

'Perhaps the deaths were natural. Though I suspect not. Vlach sorcerers are powerful adepts, and could have other ways of working their will. I have heard tales of their enemies walking off mountain ledges, as if in a trance, or being struck down where they stood, as if by lightning.'

Nightingale finished his coffee. 'I need to find them, and very soon.'

Father Mihail sighed. 'I wish I could help, but I have no idea who these people might be, or where to find them.'

'Can this ritual be performed anywhere?'

'In theory yes, but in practice the adept will always operate under cover of darkness, and use a deconsecrated church. This adds incredible strength to any ritual.'

'There can't be many of those around here.'

Father Mihail smiled. 'You'd be very surprised at exactly how many there are, especially in Norfolk. You were standing in one, just thirty minutes ago. Though of course, it has been reconsecrated now.'

'Is there a set time for this?'

'No, though as I said, the hours of darkness are preferred.'

Nightingale looked at his watch. Just after five. 'So I could have around twenty-five hours to live?'

Father Mihail's frown deepened. 'Or maybe much less. You said your names were listed in the book under Friday's date.'

'Yes.'

'If the ritual is started at midnight, it will end a few minutes later. On Friday morning.'

'Oh shit.'

'It seems you have no time to waste, my friend.'

'You genuinely think I could be in that much danger?'

'It really all depends if you believe in such things, Jack.'

'Do you?'

'Oh yes. Definitely.'

Nightingale's mobile sounded as he walked back towards the car park. No number showed on the display, but he couldn't afford to ignore anything at this stage. 'Yes?'

'Nightingale, where the Hell are you?'

It was Chalmers but Nightingale was in no mood to cooperate. 'Who wants to know?'

'You know damn well. I want that book back. Where are you?'

'I'll drop it into the station tomorrow, Chalmers. Your fault for leaving it behind.'

'You better hope you're still around to do that. Somebody seems to think you'll be brown bread by then. And where's your secretary? I sent Mason round to your shitty little office and the place was locked up.'

'I gave her the day off.'

'Don't give me that. And what do you know about a break-in at Dixon's house last night?'

'Me, nothing? Why would I?'

'Because it's just the sort of thing you would do. Where are you?'

'I'm out on a case. So what progress have you made investigating the names in the book?'

'None of your business, this is an active police investigation, and I'm not about to discuss it with a civilian who might be a suspect. Or possibly a victim.'

'You sound pleased at the prospect, Chalmers.'

'I won't lose sleep over it, that's for sure. Listen, Nightingale, I can tell you this much. We did look at the other names in that book. Some of them appear to have been former colleagues of hers. Others have no known connection to Dixon, or his wife that we can find. Quite a few very common names in there. But we managed to find six deaths that matched one of the names and the dates that were given.'

'Murders?'

'No. Natural death or accidents, the whole lot of them.'

'So they could have been written in after the event?'

'Of course. Except Dixon. And you two.'

'Yeah, I spotted that. Changing the subject, what's happened with Lucy Clarke's daughter? Is she with her dad?'

'Why?'

'I thought maybe I could go and see him.'

'Why?'

'I was the last person to see his wife. I thought he might have some questions.'

'About how she jumped in front of a train? What questions could he possibly have?'

'It's about closure, Chalmers. People need closure. You know that as well as I do.'

The Superintendent sighed, then gave Nightingale an address in Notting Hill.

'Now, I've given you something, how about you return the favour. Start with telling me where you are.'

Nightingale gave a long low whistle.

'Sorry...almers...bad...al...eaking...up.'

He pressed the red button and ended the call.

CHAPTER 23

The Grange Guest House seemed pleasant enough, though Nightingale wasn't anticipating sleeping there. But the room came with a decent en-suite bathroom, so a thorough shower was no problem. This time the map on the floor was a large-scale map of the local area, and he was once again trying to locate Catherine Dixon. The crystal swung to the right and downwards, and finally settled over a small village near the coast, which bore the unlikely name of Lower Wilverton St Thomas. There was no church marked there, but then if it had been abandoned, there probably wouldn't be.

He tried again, this time searching for Jenny. The result was the same. If the crystal was doing its job, Mrs Dixon and Jenny were together.

Nightingale put the crystal back into its bag, and shoved it into the pocket of his raincoat. He dressed quickly, in black jeans, black sweater and black trainers, put the used ritual items back into his holdall, and left the Grange just forty minutes after he'd checked in.

If there was a church in Lower Wilverton, it was possible that Father Mihail might know about it, and might be willing to come along. Nightingale was feeling out of his depth and could use all the help he could get. The priest's mobile phone was turned off, as it well might be if he was officiating, or whatever it might be that Orthodox priests did. There was just a chance that Nightingale might find him at Saint Savas. He parked opposite the church and walked quickly across the road.

He pulled the old wooden door open and stopped in his tracks, his jaw dropping in horror. Father Mihail was halfway down the church, swinging by his neck from a long gold and white sash, which had been looped around one of the beams holding the roof to the side walls. One look at the angle of his neck told Nightingale that there'd be no point calling an ambulance. It looked as if the priest had climbed up onto the back of one of the 'stacidia', thrown one end of the sash around the beam, then knotted both ends round his neck before jumping. He'd been quite a heavy man, so the drop had been quite enough to break his neck.

There was nothing Nightingale could do for the man, so he turned and left the church, hoping that there'd been nobody around to see him enter or leave. He'd only known father Mihail for a couple of hours, but had liked the man. Yet again, it seemed that anyone who came into contact with Nightingale found their luck changing for the worse. Nightingale couldn't stop himself from wondering if the priest might still be alive if he'd never met him.

'Not my fault,' he muttered to himself. 'Not my fault.'

CHAPTER 24

The moon was still full and bright as Nightingale parked the MGB on the verge of the narrow lane that led up to the ruin of St Thomas's Church. A quick stop at the local pub had produced directions and a few guffaws from the locals.

'Planning on getting married?'

'You'll be waiting a long time for the next service, bor.'

'Anyone seen the vicar lately?'

After the joking had dried up they had come up with directions to the deconsecrated church. Nightingale had forced a weak smile, thanked them, and headed back to his car.

The old church stood nearly a mile away from the last house in the village, though a few other ruins along the way suggested that it had not always been so isolated. It had obviously been abandoned hundreds of years ago. There was no trace of a roof over the nave, though the walls were still pretty much complete. A tribute to the skills of the ancient stone masons. At the far end of the nave stood a stone tower, which might have held the altar in centuries gone past. Nightingale's knowledge of church architecture was pretty sketchy.

As he walked closer, he saw light flickering from the bottom of the tower, as a figure seemed to move in front of some candles. He ducked into the shadow that the walls provided from the moonlight, and edged closer, slowly and cautiously, one tentative step at a time, alert for any sound.

By the time he was forty feet away, he could see the figure clearly. It wore a dark robe, and was bent over a small table, on which stood a metal bowl, into which the figure sprinkled something and then poured in a liquid from a small bottle. Behind the figure was a wooden lectern on which stood a huge book, closed for the moment.

As his eyes grew better accustomed to the flickering candlelight, Nightingale was able to make out another figure, standing motionless to the left of the lectern. Dressed in what looked like jeans and thin sweater, and staring straight ahead out into the nave.

Jenny.

He felt a sharp jab in his kidneys and grunted in pain.

'That was a twelve-bore shotgun,' said a soft voice behind him. 'I'm now two feet behind you. At this distance it would blow a very large hole in you. Keep your hands in your pockets, and walk slowly towards the altar. Don't look round. That's it. Now stop.'

Nightingale stood motionless, about ten feet from the figure in the grey cloak. From behind him, a second figure in a grey cloak moved to join the first, the shotgun now trained on his stomach. The first figure pulled back the hood of the cloak, shook long blonde hair free, and smiled at him.

'Jack Nightingale, I assume,' she said. 'We were told you would be joining us, but we were beginning to think you'd never arrive.' Her English was perfect though there was a trace of an East European accent.

'Dara Tasić, I presume?'

'I prefer my own name of Ilić. I assume you have met my husband.'

'Yeah. I'd have been here sooner if he'd been more helpful.'

'That would have been difficult for him, he has no idea of my...other life. He thinks I am nursing at the hospital tonight. It was a useful fiction, when I needed to be busy.'

'A priest seems an odd choice of husband for a witch.'

She laughed.

'An old-fashioned term, but it will suffice. He was harmless, but the marriage was not of my choice, I serve a higher power, and do not question its commands. He served a purpose, I carry inside me a daughter to continue the Vlach line, and to learn our craft. And now the time for husbands has passed, and we move on to a new life and greater power. '

'Are you going to finish the introductions?'

Still holding the shotgun level with the right hand, the second figure swept the left up to the hood and pushed it back. This time the long hair was dark.

Nightingale groaned as he realised who it was. 'Catherine Dixon. The devoted wife.'

'Katarina Ilić.'

'The distant cousin?'

'The very close sister.'

'It seems that the husband is always the last to know,' said Nightingale. 'But I should have guessed.'

'It was the way it was commanded,' said Katarina. 'He too was to provide me with daughters for our cause. Sadly he was incapable of fathering children, so became dispensable, once his part in the plan was done.'

'What plan?' asked Nightingale.

This time it was Dara who spoke. 'Why, to bring you to this place, Jack Nightingale.'

'But why?'

'To witness the death of Jenny McLean. And then to die yourself, in utter despair.'

Nightingale felt every hair on the back of his neck stand up in horror. 'But why? What have Jenny and I done to you? Why would you go to all these lengths?'

'I have told you, we serve a higher power. We have been given everything we wish in life, and will be given far, far more in the years to come. In return we practise our craft in safety, remove those who stand in our way, and obey the commands we are given.'

Nightingale stood in silence, trying to take in the horror of what she had just said. His mind raced back through the events of the last three days, and he realised how he'd been guided along this path at every step of the way, by forces far stronger than himself. He shuddered as the question rose in his mind of exactly how long ago this whole plan had been conceived.

But then, hadn't she told him that time had no meaning? The image of her dark eyes seemed to burn inside him, and he pictured her there, with her dark fringe, the long leather coat, and the ever present hellhound. Perhaps there really was no escape from her vengeance.

Dara was speaking again.

'Let us proceed. The Eagle must be summoned,' she said.

Nightingale looked at Jenny, who still stood motionless six feet from him, her eyes unfocused and staring straight ahead.

'What have you done to her?' he asked.

'Very little,' said Dara. 'Merely placed her under my will.'

'Hypnotised?'

'A crude term, but it will suffice. She was an easy subject, almost as if she were well used to being influenced.'

Nightingale shuddered at a memory he'd tried hard to repress. At least Jenny wouldn't know what was going to happen to her.

Dara smiled and shook her head.

'Oh no, Jack Nightingale. That would never do. I shall release her from my influence shortly, so she may feel every slash of beak and talon as the spirit of the Carpathian Eagle tears her apart. And you will feel each wound with her, powerless to help.'

'Let her go, this is about me, not her.'

'Of course it is, but she will die, and you will howl in anguish. Now be silent.'

Nightingale bit his tongue, and mentally measured the distance to the shotgun. Not a hope, but maybe if he rushed her, one quick blast would be preferable to the horror ahead. Except that would still leave Jenny at their mercy.

Dara opened the large book on the lectern, and Nightingale saw that the pages she had turned to were blank. She threw some herbs into a small metal bowl, then picked up a long copper knife. She used it to prick her finger, and squeezed in two drops of blood. She threw her head back and shouted a chant in a language Nightingale had never heard.

'Oschi, oschi, Scaraoschi! Cu gura sa te invat, cu ochii sa nu te vad.'

She repeated the phrase three times, then flung one last handful of herbs into the bowl. Golden smoke began to pour upwards, and Nightingale heard the fluttering of huge wings above his head.

'The Spirit of the Carpathian eagle has been summoned, it soars above us. It waits my guidance. It will not return to its nest until it has killed and tasted blood. I shall release her, and write her name in the book in my own blood, and then he will strike. But first, I have been commanded to wait exactly two minutes, so you may think of what lies ahead.'

She fell silent, and looked towards the back of the ruined church. Nightingale followed her gaze, but saw nothing. Or was there the hint of two figures, almost human, and almost animal back there? A voice came to his ears. Or was it in his head?

'All you have to do is call me, Nightingale. No spells, just ask me to help you, and you know I will. Just ask. Just call my name.'

But he knew the price he'd have to pay. Was anything worth that?

Now there was another voice in his head, weaker, but still clear. Mrs Steadman. 'No, Mr Nightingale. Darkness can never drive out darkness. Only the Light can do that. The Light, Mr Nightingale. The Light...'

'Silence. Begone, old woman. He is mine, call on me, Nightingale. I can help you. Call on me, call on me.'

Nightingale closed his eyes and shook his head. The voices were gone now, and Nightingale stared back at the book, a choice of paths ahead of him.

'Wake up, Jenny, 'said Dara.

The effect was immediate. Jenny's eyes focused, she looked round in terror and started shivering.

'Jack, where are we? What's happening? I'm so cold.'

'Stand still, Jenny,' said Nightingale.

'She cannot move,' said Dara. 'Now, the time has come.' She took up a long pointed feather and the knife again. This time she drew the knife across the palm of her hand, and blood oozed out immediately. She rubbed it against the feather, until the tip was covered in her blood. She picked up something from the table, and held it up. Nightingale recognised it as Jenny's mobile. She touched it against the page of the book.

Katarina spoke. 'Give me my book, Jack Nightingale. I sense you have it here, and I would not have it damaged.'

Dara had written the first four letters of Jenny's name, and was squeezing out more blood.

Nightingale fumbled in his raincoat pocket and took out Katarina's book, still in the evidence bag. He held it up.

'Take it out of that bag and place it gently on the ground in front of you,' said Katarina, as Dara reached the 'L' of Jenny's surname.

Nightingale did as he was told.

As he straightened up he heard Mrs Steadman's voice. 'The crystal, Mr Nightingale. The crystal has the Light.'

Nightingale stared at Dara, watching like a hawk for the split second when her eyes left him and looked down greedily at the book. He put his right hand into his raincoat pocket and eased the crystal out of its leather pouch. It was warm to the touch and felt as if it was pulsing to match the beat of his heart.

The moment came. Dara looked down at the book.

Nightingale's right hand was instantly out of his pocket, and he threw the crystal at the book. The moment it touched the page, there was a blinding flash of pink light, and pink flames shot from the book, straight into Dara's face. She screamed in agony, there was an appalling screech from above him and a deafening flapping of giant wings. Nightingale leapt at Jenny, pulled her to the ground, and lay across her in a desperate attempt to shield her.

The awful screeching continued, as did the flapping of wings and the screams of the two women seemed as if they would never end.

Silence fell eventually.

Nightingale stayed prone for a further three minutes or so, his heart racing, his skin covered in sweat. Jenny seemed to have fainted, but he could feel her breathing. Finally he got up. The moon had gone behind a cloud, but he pulled a small torch from his pocket, and shone it around.

It took every ounce of his self control not to vomit.

The two women had been literally disembowelled, and pieces of flesh and entrails were everywhere. The large book had been reduced to ashes, and all that was left of the pink crystal was a lump of carbon. The small book had burned with such fury that it was just a mass of melted leather and plastic. Nightingale picked it up, put it back into the evidence bag and shoved it in his pocket. He wasn't looking forward to seeing Chalmers tomorrow and telling him that he'd lost it.

Jenny was still pretty much out of it, but he managed to drag and carry her back to the MGB. He hoped she wouldn't come around for a while. It might give him chance to think of exactly what he was going to tell her. He eased her into the passenger seat and then climbed in next to her. The car started first time, he pointed it at London and put his foot down.

He didn't see the young girl in the black leather raincoat walk through the church ruins and gaze at the mess on the ground with her dark unblinking eyes.. The dog by her side was chewing enthusiastically on something. She looked down at the animal.

'It's so hard to get good help these days, isn't it boy?'

The dog looked up at her with featureless black eyes and wagged its tail. She looked across the fields at the red tail-lights of the MGB as they disappeared into the night.

'So, white wins this time, and the pawns go back into the box until the next round. But soon it will be black's turn to win. I shall have your soul, I promise you.'

She bared her pointed teeth in a feral snarl.

'You're going to Hell, Jack Nightingale. And there's nothing that bitch Steadman can do to stop it.'

CHAPTER 25

Nightingale drove Jenny home. By the time he pulled up in front of her mews house she was awake, but still drowsy and confused. He helped her out of the car and she fumbled in her pocket and pulled out the door keys. Nightingale unlocked the door and helped her inside. Her burglar alarm system began to beep but he knew the security code and tapped in the four digits to silence it.

He put her down on the sofa and went to the kitchen to get her a glass of water, which she gulped down. 'What happened back there?' she asked.

'How much do you remember?'

She frowned. 'Nothing since they grabbed me.'

'To be honest, it's better that we leave it that way.'

She forced a smile. 'It was bad?'

Nightingale nodded. 'Yeah, it was bad. You don't remember anything?'

She shook her head. 'There was a knock on the door, first thing. There was this woman there who said she was doing some sort of survey and then she plunged a hypodermic into my neck and that's pretty much the last thing I remember.'

'They took you to Norwich and summoned that bird thing.'

'The bird thing being the eagle of death?'

'Yeah.'

'And you what? Killed it?'

'No. I'm not sure how you'd go about killing it. But I managed to destroy the books that they were using.' He reached into his raincoat pocket and took out the remains of the book in the evidence bag. He gave it to her and her eyes widened in astonishment.

'As unlikely as that sounds, yes. Mrs Steadman had given me a crystal. The crystal was from the Light, the eagle was from the Dark.'

'So they cancelled each other out? Like matter and anti-matter?'

Nightingale chuckled. 'That's exactly what I said. And yeah, that's what happened.' He took the remains of the book from her and put it back in his pocket.

'Chalmers won't be happy about that,' said Jenny, nodding at his pocket.

Nightingale shrugged. 'I'll cross that bridge when I come to it,' he said. 'The problem is, I can't really tell him what happened because there's no way he'd believe it.'

'The crystal killed the eagle?'

Nightingale shook his head. 'No, the crystal destroyed the books. But the eagle had to be told who or what to kill, and when that guidance wasn't forthcoming it killed the people who summoned it. That was one of the rules – it couldn't return to its nest until it has killed and tasted blood.' He smiled. 'It's always the small print that catches you out in the end.'

'But it won't come back?'

'It might if someone else summons it. But the books are destroyed so our names are no longer in the frame.'

He patted her on the shoulder and stood. 'You need to rest,' he said. 'You might as well take tomorrow morning off. It's not as if we've got much on at the moment.'

'Thanks,' she said, then frowned. 'Wait a minute, tomorrow's Saturday.'

'All the better,' he said. 'You can have the whole day off, can't you.'

'It's called the weekend, Jack.'

'Well I've got things to do,' said Nightingale. 'I'm sure Chalmers will be chasing me for an update. And I need to go and see Lucy Clarke's ex-husband.'

Jenny frowned. 'Lucy Clarke?'

'The woman who killed herself at the Tube station. She wants me to talk to her ex-husband and her daughter. She wants them to know that she didn't kill herself and that she loves them.'

Jenny looked pained. 'That's going to be a difficult conversation to have.'

'Another bridge I'll have to cross. Are you going to be okay?'

She nodded. 'I'm tired. But other than that I'm fine. You be careful out there, okay?'

Stephen Leather

Nightingale grinned. 'Always,' he said.

He let himself out of the house, climbed into his MGB and drove off. He didn't see the good looking man with black hair and dark blue eyes standing in the shadows at the end of the mews. The man smiled as the MGB drove away. 'Soon, Nightingale,' whispered the man. 'Sooner than you think.'

CHAPTER 26

Nightingale yawned and looked up at the sign announcing the arrival times of the Central line trains. Two minutes, seven minutes and eleven minutes. He wanted a cigarette but smoking was most definitely not allowed at Tube stations and the network of CCTV cameras meant that any transgression would be dealt with promptly and expensively. The last time he had checked, the fine was £1,000. He patted his pocket. His nicotine hit could wait.

He looked up at the electronic sign again. One minute. He still hadn't worked out what he was going to say to Mr Clarke. Or to Charlie. He looked at his watch. He had just over half an hour to think of something. He could maybe pass himself off as a psychic or a spiritualist and say that he had a message for them, that Lucy had spoken to him from beyond the grave. It wasn't the truth, of course, but would they believe the truth, that he had spoken to her in a dark mirror? If he told them that then they'd maybe want to try it for themselves, and Nightingale knew that was a bad idea. Nothing good ever came of talking to the dead. The dead were dead and best left that way.

A figure appeared at Nightingale's left shoulder. He could never understand the urge to rush to board a train that hadn't even arrived, but that was often the way with many Londoners. Rush, rush, bloody rush. Nightingale shuffled to the side. The figure shuffled with him, and that annoyed the hell out of Nightingale. He turned. It was a man, just over six feet tall and wearing a dark overcoat over a suit. Nightingale flashed the man an angry look but the man smiled amiably. He had perfect white teeth and eyes that were a blue so dark that they were almost black.

Nightingale looked away. To his right were a young couple of denim-wearing teenagers making out, oblivious to the judgmental looks being thrown their way. The man moved closer to Nightingale, then leant towards him so that his mouth was only inches away from Nightingale's ear. The Tannoy burst into life announcing the arrival of the next train and that passengers needed to move back from the edge of the platform. The announcement was almost certainly aimed at the teenagers who had strayed over the yellow line as they locked lips, but they were oblivious.

The man was even closer to Nightingale now. 'Did you hear what I just said?' asked the man, his forehead creased into a frown. Nightingale could smell mint on the man's breath.

Nightingale grinned. 'Sorry, mate, I can't hear a thing,' he said.

A blast of air on his right cheek announced the imminent arrival of the train. The man gripped Nightingale's arms with fingers that felt like talons. His lips drew back in a snarl and he pulled Nightingale towards him. Nightingale felt warm breath on his ear as the man spoke earnestly. Nightingale laughed and the grip tightened on his arm. Nightingale turned. The eyes were completely black now. The teeth were no longer gleaming white, they were yellowed and pointed like fangs. The breath that seeped from between the thing's cruel lips was fetid and smelled of sulphur. The train roared out of the tunnel. Nightingale twisted his arm away from whatever it was that was holding him, then he grabbed it by the lapels of its coat, twisted it around and then hurled it off the platform and into the path of the oncoming train. The brakes were already screeching but the train was still moving quickly and the body disappeared under the cab without making a sound.

The train came to a halt as the passengers around Nightingale screamed. He figured it would only be a matter of time before someone grabbed him and there was every chance that he would end up on the ground on the receiving end of a kick or two. He reached up his hands and pulled the foam earplugs from his ears. As he slipped the earplugs into their plastic case and put the case into the pocket of his raincoat, the first shouts started.

'He did it!'

'That bastard in the raincoat pushed him!'

'He killed him, Get him!'

'Get that scum now and call the fucking cops!'

A hand grabbed him by the shoulder and someone kicked his feet away from under him. Nightingale managed to break his fall so he didn't hit the platform too hard. 'Here we go again,' he muttered as he curled up into a foetal ball.

CHAPTER 27

This time they left Nightingale in an interview room for the best part of four hours, initially under the watchful eye of a middle-aged uniformed constable who clearly thought he had better things to do. Several times Nightingale tried to start a conversation but the constable said nothing. The uniformed constable was replaced after three hours by a younger version who was equally uncommunicative. Nightingale figured they had been ordered not to talk to him. He settled back in his chair, stretched out his legs and tried to ignore his full bladder and parched throat.

Eventually Chalmers appeared, again in full uniform and this time accompanied by a young woman wearing a blazer and dark trousers. Chalmers closed the door and gestured at the woman. 'This is DC Annette Fisher, she's recently joined us so I wanted to introduce her to the notorious Jack Nightingale.'

Nightingale nodded and smiled at her. 'How's it going?'

'So far, so good,' she said.

'Did they offer you a coffee?' Chalmers asked him as he sat down at the opposite side of the table.

Nightingale wondered if he was joking. 'No,' he said, frowning as he tried to think what the punch line would be.

'I'm sure DC Fisher wouldn't mind popping to the canteen for you.' The superintendent looked at the detective. 'Would you? I hate asking but we can hardly let Mr Nightingale wander around the station.'

'Not a problem, Sir,' said Fisher, and she left the room.

Chalmers settled back in his chair. 'Lovely girl,' he said. 'Very keen.'

'That's sexist, Chalmers. And sending her for coffee was sexist too.'

'I wanted her to meet you, but I need a chat with you in private. So two birds, right?'

'I'm not sure that makes any sense, but go ahead.'

The superintendent nodded slowly, his eyes staring at Nightingale with almost clinical interest. 'So you're now making a habit of pushing people under trains?'

'I didn't push Lucy Clarke. I tried to grab her.'

'And today?'

'Today is complicated.'

'So you're not denying that you pushed a man under a train this morning?'

'Was the station CCTV working?' asked Nightingale.

'It was indeed.' Chalmers grinned.

'Then maybe I should be cautioned and maybe I should ask for a lawyer.'

'That would be one way to go, of course. You know the Police and Criminal Evidence Act as well as I do. Did you know the man?'

Nightingale shook his head.

'So he was a stranger? Why would you push a stranger under a train, Nightingale?'

'As I said, it's complicated.'

'So you're not denying it?'

'You've got the CCTV.'

'Why don't you try to explain what happened before DC Fisher gets back.

'You won't believe me, Chalmers.'

'Try me.'

Nightingale folded his arms and sighed. He really wanted a cigarette but from the way things were going he figured it would be a long time before he was allowed to light up again. There was no story that he could spin that Chalmers would believe. This wasn't a situation he could lie his way out of. All he could do was to tell the truth. He sighed. 'Okay, fine. Those suicides you've been looking at, some sort of demon from Hell has been behind them. They call it The Whisper Man. He gets close to you and he whispers in your ear and not long afterwards you kill yourself.'

The superintendent's face stayed impassive but his eyes hardened.

'It came for me on the platform. I fought back. It went under the train.'

'It's a demon?'

'Yes.'

'From Hell?'

'Yes?'

'And you killed it by pushing it under a train? Bollocks. You need silver bullets or a stake through the heart.'

'If you want to kill a werewolf or a vampire, sure. But this was a demon that takes human form, and when it's in human form it can be killed the same way you or I can be killed.'

Chalmers continued to stare at Nightingale. 'So this thing whispers in your ear and you kill yourself?'

'Pretty much, yeah.'

'So why are you sitting here looking like shit and not smeared over the rails?'

Nightingale wrinkled his nose. He knew that the story he was telling made almost no sense at all, and that there was no way Chalmers was going to believe a word of it. But he was even less likely to believe that the only reason he had survived was because Proserpine had warned him.

'I was wearing earplugs,' he said eventually.

'You were what?'

'Earplugs. I live in Bayswater, it's noisy, sometimes I sleep with earplugs in. This morning I forgot to take them out.'

Chalmers shook his head. 'Do you think I'm stupid?'

Nightingale reached into his pocket and took out a small clear plastic case containing two orange earplugs.'

'Bullshit,' said Chalmers.

Nightingale shrugged and put the case back in his pocket.

Chalmers glared at him for several seconds, then nodded slowly. 'That is one hell of a story, Nightingale.'

Nightingale shrugged. 'Take it or leave it,' he said. 'But you have to realise that I wouldn't push a complete stranger under the wheels of a train.'

'Except that was exactly what you did.'

'If I hadn't, I'd be dead.' Nightingale ran his hands through his hair. 'I think I need a solicitor now if you're going to charge me.'

'Charge you with what?'

Nightingale lowered his arms, confused. 'You've got CCTV of me pushing a man under a train. I assume no matter what I say, I'm going to be put on trial.'

'This Whisper Man, when it appeared to you, what did it look like?'

Nightingale frowned. 'You've got the CCTV, right?'

'The face is blurred,' said Chalmers. 'Your face is okay, the faces of everyone else on the platform are okay, but the man, as I said, his face is blurred. We can't even see if he is talking to you. We can see what he's wearing, but we can't see his face.'

'Did you see a Goth girl, with a dog?'

'What the hell are you talking about, Nightingale? There was no Goth girl on the platform. Are you trying to fix up some sort of insanity plea?'

'I sound crazy, don't I?'

Chalmers nodded. 'No question of that. And I doubt anyone is going to believe that Whisper Man story.'

'Maybe,' said Nightingale. 'But I'm fairly sure that you won't be having any more unexplained suicides.'

'So all's well that ends well?'

Nightingale forced a smile. 'Except for the fact that I'm going to be charged with murder.'

Chalmers flashed him a complicated smile. 'Well, on that score, as you say, it's complicated.'

Nightingale tilted his head on one side. 'What's going on, Chalmers?'

'I wish I knew, Nightingale,' said the superintendent. 'There's no one I'd like to see standing in the dock more than you, but for that we need a body and...' He shrugged.

Nightingale leaned forward. 'There's no body?'

'It's the strangest thing,' said Chalmers. 'The CCTV clearly shows the man going in front of the train. Plenty of eyewitnesses saw you push him to his death.'

'Allegedly,' said Nightingale.

Chalmers ignored the interruption. 'The station was closed and then the train was moved back. But there was nothing there,

Nightingale. No body, no blood, no DNA, no sign that anyone had ever been underneath the train. It's as if it never happened.'

Nightingale shook his head, trying to clear his thoughts. How could there not have been a body under the train? Then realisation dawned. Without a body, the police had no case, no matter what the CCTV showed. He was in the clear. A smile slowly spread across his face. 'Thank you Proserpine,' he muttered under his breath. 'I owe you one,'

'What was that?' said Chalmers.

Nightingale grinned. 'Nothing,' he said.

The door opened and DC Fisher reappeared holding a cup of coffee. Chalmers smiled up at her. 'Mr Nightingale will be having that to go, as the Americans say,' he said.

Printed in Great Britain
by Amazon

27631820R00067